It w...
In the ...
Patrice and T.K. kissed tenderly.
He ran his lips down her neck, stopping
at the crevice where her breasts
came together in the corset she wore.

Patrice trembled with pleasure. Rehearsal aside, she was turned on by T.K. He slowly removed her corset and her breasts fell into his big hands. Patrice unbuttoned T.K.'s shirt and ran her hands over his smooth, muscular chest. She felt herself growing moist between her legs, so she tried to focus her mind elsewhere.

She closed her eyes and T.K. kissed her. She didn't recall a kiss being in the script at this point.

The script. She tried to focus on the script. How Bella gestured without speaking, indicating where she wanted Bass to touch her. She could do that. In Bella she'd found free expression. It was almost like making love to T.K. When they mimicked full-on intercourse, there was a thick cloth between them, but they were each naked from the waist up, and their chests were rubbing. What she did for art. They screamed in ecstasy, and it was over. They fell onto the bed, exhausted but satisfied.

The director yelled, "Cut!"

Books by Janice Sims

Kimani Romance

Temptation's Song
Temptation's Kiss

JANICE SIMS

is the author of eighteen novels and has had stories included in nine anthologies. She is the recipient of an Emma Award for her novel *Desert Heat* and two Romance in Color awards. She also received an Award of Excellence for her novel *For Keeps* and a Best Novella award for her short story in the anthology *A Very Special Love.* She lives in central Florida with her family.

TEMPTATION'S
Kiss

JANICE SIMS

KIMANI
ROMANCE

To the readers who have been with me since
Affair of the Heart. And to the new readers who just
decided to try one of my books for the first time. You're
both the reason I stay up late at night writing. Thank you!

 KIMANI PRESS™

Recycling programs
for this product may
not exist in your area.

ISBN-13: 978-0-373-86210-8

TEMPTATION'S KISS

Copyright © 2011 by Janice Sims

All rights reserved. The reproduction, transmission or utilization
of this work in whole or in part in any form by any electronic, mechanical
or other means, now known or hereafter invented, including xerography,
photocopying and recording, or in any information storage or retrieval
system, is forbidden without written permission. For permission please
contact Kimani Press, Editorial Office, 233 Broadway, New York, NY
10279 U.S.A.

This is a work of fiction. Names, characters, places and incidents are
either the product of the author's imagination or are used fictitiously,
and any resemblance to actual persons, living or dead, business establishments,
events or locales is entirely coincidental.

® and TM are trademarks. Trademarks indicated with ® are registered in
the United States Patent and Trademark Office, the Canadian Trade Marks
Office and/or other countries.

www.kimanipress.com

Printed in U.S.A.

Dear Reader,

While writing *Temptation's Kiss* I finally understood exactly why you hear about so many actors falling in love on the set of a film. In the book, Patrice and T.K. have a hard time denying their passion for one another. And being constantly thrown together on the set of the movie they are shooting only makes them want each other even more.

And by the way, the character T.K. portrays in the movie, Frontier Marshal Bass Reeves, really existed.

Look for the final book in the trilogy, *Dance of Temptation,* in a store near you soon. Write to me at jani569432@aol.com, or visit my website at www.janicesims.com. You can also find me on Facebook. And if you're not online yet you can write me at P.O. Box 811, Mascotte, FL 34753-0811.

Best always,

Janice Sims

ACKNOWLEDGMENTS

Thanks to my editor, Kelli Martin,
for her help in making this book the best it could
possibly be. And to the rest of the editorial staff at
Kimani Press, including Alex Colon, who gave me
computer tips. You're all wonderful to work with.

Chapter 1

Sweat trickled between Patrice Sutton's brows. She wiped it off and dried her damp palm on the leg of her jeans. Her gaze was on the woman ahead of her in the calf-roping competition as she climbed onto her horse and prepared to race out of the box after the calf when it was released from the chute.

Suddenly someone yanked on her shirtsleeve. She peered underneath the brim of her cowboy hat to see that it was her younger sister, Keira. "Patty, no matter what you do, you've got to beat Lucy's time," Keira said urgently.

Patrice laughed. "This is a charity event, not an actual competition. I'm here to help raise money for the kids. Besides, it's hot as Hades today. I doubt if I'll beat her time."

The rodeo, which was held every July in Albuquerque, New Mexico, benefited a local children's hospital. The stadium was filled with kids who were out of school for the summer. Patrice was an up-and-coming film star due to a now-canceled sitcom of some acclaim and starring roles in two successful action films.

"Please, Patty," Keira whined. "There's no time to tell you why now, but it's for a good reason." Patrice smiled. Keira sounded the way she had when she was a little girl.

Looking at her petite sister, Patrice pursed her lips, thinking. "Lucy's got the best time so far, at ten seconds. That's pretty good seeing as how some professional ropers come in at seven. She competes in these events year-round. I haven't competed since high school."

Frustrated, Keira blew air between full lips. "Yeah, but you ride as often as you can fit it into your schedule, and I know you've been practicing like crazy since you've been home. Ma told me. You used to beat Lucy all the time when you were both on the local circuit."

The announcer's voice came over the loudspeaker. "Oops, that's okay, Mary Jane, better luck next time. Folks, Mary Jane got a cowboy speeding ticket because her horse broke the barrier before his time. So that sets Mary Jane's time at 21 seconds. Miss Lucy Lopez is still the rider to beat."

The crowd of nearly twelve hundred spectators cheered for Lucy Lopez.

"If she wins," hissed Keira, "I'll never hear the end of it."

"That's your sister-in-law you're talking about," Patrice said teasingly.

A cowboy in a black hat, denim shirt, jeans, black boots and leather chaps motioned for Patrice to follow him. It was time for her to mount her horse. "Gotta go," said Patrice to her still-fuming sister.

"You've got too much of a competitive spirit to lie down and take it," Keira yelled at Patrice's back.

Patrice mounted her favorite quarter horse, Billy One Star. He was named this because of the white mark under his forelock. He was a handsome, healthy three-year-old. Her parents had given him to her on her twenty-fifth birthday last year.

She patted his muscular neck as she envisioned the next few minutes, mentally preparing herself. Her heart thudded with excitement. Like she'd told Keira, she hadn't competed in years. She was nervous. However, she stayed in shape, and she rode Billy One Star as often as she could get home between gigs. Life as an actress who was trying to limit her roles to films gave her quite a lot of downtime between projects.

Billy One Star was so well trained that he didn't move a muscle after Patrice signaled to the chute operator that she was ready and the calf went running out of the chute. The rider was supposed to give the calf a running start before going after him, and Patrice waited the appropriate amount of time before signaling to Billy One Star to do his thing. Billy's powerful body leaped forward, and soon they were racing after the calf at his top speed. Patrice concentrated, mouth boxed in determination, as she threw the lariat and looped it around the calf's neck. She then signaled to Billy to stop, and the horse abruptly skidded to a stop. She leaped from his back, quickly laid the calf onto its side and snared three of its legs together in a wrap and a slap, or a half-hitch knot.

She threw her hands in the air denoting she was done. Billy slowly backed away from the calf in order to maintain the tautness of the rope until Patrice could climb onto his back again and move forward to relax the rope on the calf.

"Ooh, wee!" exclaimed the announcer. "That little filly knows her roping. Ms. Patrice Sutton, Albuquerque girl and TV-and-screen star, caught that 'lil doggie in nine seconds flat. It's the new time to beat, buckaroos!"

The crowd roared. Patrice waved her hat in the air and signaled Billy One Star to take a bow as she'd taught him. Billy bowed by lowering his great head and bending his front legs slightly.

A couple of cowboys detached Patrice's lariat from the calf and untied the calf, who immediately got to its feet, unhurt. Patrice sighed, relieved. She always worried that she might injure the calf, but in all the years she'd been roping, she had never done so.

She rode Billy out of the stadium to enthusiastic applause. When she got to the area behind the corral where various RVs and horse trailers were parked, awaiting the return of their passengers, she was greeted by her excited family. Her brother Luke took hold of Billy's bit and patted his neck while Patrice dismounted and removed her hat. She was immediately enveloped in her father's arms. "Way to go, Peanut," he said.

Patrice beamed. Nobody called her Peanut except her daddy. Patrick Sutton's handsome brown face crinkled in a grin. Six-two to Patrice's five-seven, he bent to hug her. "You should have heard your momma cheering," he said proudly, turning to look back at Cady Sutton.

"Of course I was," Cady said. Patrick released Patrice so his wife could hug her. "It brought back memories." When she was younger, Cady had been a roper, too. Patrice was the only one of her two daughters who'd shown any interest in it. She reached up to gently caress Patrice's cheek. "Well done!"

"Thank you, Momma," said Patrice, her face a mass of smiles.

Keira came running up to everyone. "You beat Lucy's time. I'm so happy."

"What was that all about?" Patrice asked, referring to Keira's earlier strange behavior.

Keira, who was slender and had skin a little lighter than Patrice's medium-brown skin, smoothed her dark auburn curls away from her heart-shaped face and grimaced. "I overheard her telling one of the other competitors that she planned to mop up the floor with Little Miss Movie Star. That's you! She said no one was going to steal her title as the area's champion lady roper, especially not the sister of the little gold digger—that's me—who had wormed her way into her brother's heart. She hates me."

"That was mean," Patrice agreed, sad that Lucy was making Keira's life difficult. "I'm here for the kids, and my career is fine, thank you!"

Her mother jumped suddenly. "Oh, my goodness, your cell phone just vibrated," she said with a laugh. She had been holding Patrice's purse for her until after she'd competed in the event.

She handed the shoulder bag to Patrice now, and Patrice quickly reached in and retrieved her still-vibrating phone. Looking down at the display, she saw that it was Blanca Mendes, her agent. "I'd better answer this."

She flipped the phone open. "Hi, Blanca. How are you?"

"Fine, fine," Blanca replied in her hurried manner. "Listen, chica, you've got to get back to L.A. as soon as possible. Mark Greenberg wants to see you in his office at 11:00 a.m. tomorrow morning."

"I just got through hog-tying a calf in a rodeo. You *do* know where I am, right?"

Blanca laughed shortly. "It's Thursday. You must be in The Land of Enchantment, otherwise known as New Mexico."

"Albuquerque is nearly eight hundred miles from Los Angeles," Patrice reminded her.

"I know that you drove home on this trip, sweetie," said Blanca. "You don't have time to drive back. I've booked you on a six o'clock flight out. Just go to the desk at your favorite airline, and they'll take care of you."

"Six o'clock!" Patrice cried. "It's already half past four."

"Then you'd better get a move on," Blanca told her. "T. K. McKenna. Need I say more?"

"No," Patrice sighed.

"That's what I thought," said her agent, satisfied she'd gotten her point across. "I've arranged to have a car pick you up at the airport. You can get a good night's rest and be refreshed for your eleven o'clock meeting. I have a good feeling about this. Mark wouldn't have asked to see you again unless he was really interested. I know how he thinks. He probably wants you to read with one of the other actors."

Patrice's heart leaped into her throat. "Do you think he wants me to read with T.K.?"

"T.K. doesn't have to audition for anyone," Blanca replied.

"But the role I'm up for is his love interest in the film," said Patrice hopefully.

"Be prepared for whatever happens," advised Blanca. "However, I seriously doubt T.K. will show up. Besides, I would prefer to have you cool, calm and collected. Even I would freak out at the prospect of meeting T.K."

Patrice laughed shortly. Blanca Mendes usually wasn't intimidated by anyone.

"Okay, I won't get my hopes up," Patrice promised. "Thanks, Blanca. I'll make that flight."

"Of course you will, chica," said Blanca, "because you understand that to get anywhere in this business one must be prepared to make—"

"—sacrifices," Patrice finished for her.

"Call me after the meeting. We'll go out and celebrate," said Blanca confidently.

Patrice closed her phone and looked into the crestfallen faces of her family. She sighed heavily. "I guess you got the gist of that. I've got to leave this afternoon."

"Did I hear you say 'T.K.'?" Keira asked excitedly, practically jumping up and down.

"That's right," Patrice told everyone. "I auditioned for the role opposite T.K. in a Western of which he's also serving as one of the producers. I didn't tell you because I didn't want you to get your hopes up for me in case I didn't get the part."

Cady put her arm about Patrice's waist. "Oh, honey, we root for you no matter what. We know you have your head on straight and realize that when you don't get a role you really want that it isn't the end of the world. Maybe something better is waiting just around the corner."

Patrice wondered what could be better than starring opposite T. K. McKenna, one of the biggest box-office draws in the world. It had to be something mighty good.

She smiled down at her mother and hugged her. "Thanks. I appreciate that."

She straightened and looked at them all in turn. "I'm sorry to have to cut my visit short."

They all shrugged aside her apology, assuring her they understood.

The announcer's voice rang out. "If the lady ropers would gather in the center of the stadium, it's time to announce the winner of the competition."

Keira grabbed Patrice by the arm. "Come on, I can't wait to see Lucy's face."

Patrice, Keira and her parents walked back to the stadium while Patrice's brother Luke led Billy One Star to his horse trailer where he would rub him down before putting him inside for the trip home, a ranch on the outskirts of Albuquerque.

Luke, twenty, was a junior in college but lived at home where he was being groomed to run the ranch when his father retired. The Suttons had been cattle ranchers in New Mexico since the late 1800s when an ancestor of Patrick's, an ex-slave also named Patrick, had left Baton Rouge, Louisiana, in search of a better way of life. He'd married a fellow Louisianan woman and soon there were Suttons spread out over New Mexico. However, because of a scarcity of blacks Sutton offspring were obliged to marry Native Americans and Mexicans. Patrice's father had quite a bit of Native American blood. Her mother hailed from South Carolina and was African-American. She had met her husband when she had taken a trip to the Southwest with girlfriends following her college graduation. The handsome rancher had swept her off her feet, and she had never returned to South Carolina to live.

* * *

Patrice closed her eyes as she relaxed against the airplane's seat. Keira had gotten her to the airport with ten minutes to spare. Luckily, she'd had no bags to check. Blanca had worked her magic, and her transition from terminal to airplane had been flawless. She smiled. It had been fun competing in a rodeo again. She had not dreamed she would actually win the competition. Keira had been happier than she was when she was handed her trophy. The sour look on Lucy Lopez's face had confirmed what Keira had said about her: she indeed had a bone to pick with Patrice.

Patrice was having none of that, though. After all, Keira was Lucy's sister-in-law. For Keira's sake, if not for anything else, there should be peace in the family. Patrice had stepped up to the microphone and said, "Thank you so much. It's my pleasure to be here today, and I'm thrilled to have won. However, I think I would be remiss if I didn't thank the wonderful women who also competed in the event, especially Ms. Lucy Lopez, who has been citywide champion for years now." She offered Lucy her hand in congratulations. Lucy shook it, an astonished expression on her pretty face.

As Patrice left the stage, she overheard one of the other women say, "That was sweet of her."

"We're related, you know," Lucy had said nonchalantly.

"Oh, yeah, how?" asked the woman, surprised.

"Her sister's married to my brother, Jorge, the doctor," said Lucy proudly.

Patrice had left feeling a bit hopeful about the future relationship of her sister and Lucy. Later, when she had told Keira about it, her sister had said, "That was just her public face. She still hates me. The test will come at the next family gathering."

Family dynamics, Patrice thought. *They're so complicated.*

Trevor Kennedy, or T.K., McKenna sat on the deck at his house in Malibu ostensibly watching the sunset but actually thinking of Malcolm, his baby brother, who had been killed in a car crash only a few months ago. Malcolm had lived with him. T.K. had given him a job as an assistant in order to keep an eye on him. Malcolm didn't have any administrative duties. He simply accompanied T.K. wherever he went whether it was to the studio, to an appointment, or on location when he worked on a film. T.K., thirty-six, had been three years older than Malcolm, but it seemed that he was many years older because Malcolm had been mildly mentally deficient. His condition had been an accident of birth. He had experienced a lack of oxygen during his delivery. To someone who didn't know him well, his mental state wasn't very noticeable. Malcolm had been a healthy, happy man with a good heart and a great sense of humor. Where his mental deficiency showed was in his relationships with people. He was so easygoing, so trusting, oftentimes people took advantage of his naivety. If he saw someone who needed a meal, he would give him money to buy food. If he knew someone who needed money, he would empty his pockets. Many times he had been tricked out of money or possessions by unscrupulous so-called friends. When it came to women, Malcolm, who had been very shy, was like putty in their hands.

This was what was troubling T.K. right now. Malcolm had been dating a woman named Aisha Jackson before his death. After he'd died, Aisha claimed that she was three months pregnant with Malcolm's child.

T.K. and his parents, Rose Kennedy McKenna and David McKenna, were not about to miss the opportunity to know Malcolm's child if it were true, so from that point on, they took care of Aisha. She moved in with Rose and David, and it was agreed that after the baby was born a DNA test would be performed to confirm that Malcolm was the father.

T.K. had a terrible feeling in the pit of his stomach that Aisha was lying, but until the baby was born, he had no way of confirming his suspicions. Some part of him hoped he would be proven wrong. He would like to be an uncle to Malcolm's child. However, he'd encountered too many opportunists since fame had swept him up in its clutches to not be cynical.

His cell phone rang, and he looked at the display. It was his friend and business partner, producer Mark Greenberg. "Hey, Mark."

"You *will* be able to make the meeting in the morning, won't you? I'd like to see you two together to see if you jibe."

T.K. smiled at Mark's use of the word *jibe*. In lots of ways, Mark was old-fashioned. Although he lived and worked in L.A., his sensibilities were that of a small-town Jewish boy from Hoboken, New Jersey. T.K. liked that about him.

"We'll only be working together, not getting married," T.K. joked. "Yeah, I'll be there."

"Did you get the chance to watch those movies I sent over?" Mark asked skeptically.

"I did," T.K. answered, surprising Mark. "The camera definitely loves her, and she can actually act."

Mark laughed. They often joked about the recent crop of actresses who were beautiful but vapid and couldn't act their way out of a paper bag, as Mark had put it.

"Yes, yes," he said now. "Patrice Sutton has it all— looks, talent and just a touch of fearlessness. I like her."

"I can tell," T.K. said, laughing softly. "What exactly do you mean by fearlessness?"

"Her agent phoned to confirm that Patrice would be at the meeting, and you'll never guess what Ms. Sutton was doing today."

T.K. hated it when someone wanted him to guess anything. He laughed. "Don't keep me in suspense!"

After Mark told him, he laughed even harder. "A sistuh?"

"That's what I said," Mark told him. "It was as unbelievable as it would have been if it were one of my sisters or cousins. I can't imagine one of those princesses in the dust and dirt chasing after a calf on horseback and jumping off said horse to throw the calf to the ground and tie its legs together. My nana would have a stroke."

"I can't wait to meet her," T.K. said sincerely.

Mark laughed. "It should be interesting."

Chapter 2

The same driver who had picked Patrice up at the airport last night drove her to Mark Greenberg's office in downtown L.A. Friday morning. The day was fairly clear, and the temperature was in the high seventies.

As she climbed from the backseat, the driver—a good-looking, tall, broad-shouldered brother with a nice 'fro and a goatee—offered her a hand out of the car. Patrice couldn't see his eyes behind his dark sunglasses as she accepted his help, but she saw his head tip downward when her skirt hitched up. He smiled. "Would you like me to wait, Ms. Sutton?"

Patrice straightened and looked up at the tall building. "No, I'll call a cab when I'm ready to leave," she told him. "Thank you."

"It's been my pleasure," he said.

Patrice smoothed the skirt of her off-white sleeveless A-line dress. It's hem fell about three inches above her shapely knees, and the bodice didn't reveal a great deal of cleavage. Brown leather designer pumps and a shoulder bag completed her ensemble. She looked smart and sexy all at once. Tinted glass concealed the lobby from outside eyes, so she was pleasantly surprised by the understated elegance of Italian tile on the lobby's floor, contemporary furnishings that looked welcoming instead of intimidating and gleaming black granite on the reception desk. The woman behind the desk was a brunette in her mid-thirties. People milled about the lobby, but there was no one presently at the desk. Patrice stepped up to it. "Good morning, I have an appointment to see Mark Greenberg."

The woman looked her up and down, her light-colored brown eyes openly assessing her and appearing to find her wanting. She wrinkled her nose as if she smelled something bad. "What is your name, please?"

"Patrice Sutton," said Patrice with a warm smile. Over the years she'd been dismissed by so many receptionists that the woman's attitude didn't faze her. Half the time, even if they knew exactly who you were, they would still make you wait—or at the very least, draw out the time you had to stand there while they verified your identity.

Patrice had run two miles that morning, though, and she was still feeling the endorphins coursing through her. They were a wonderful mood-enhancing drug. A receptionist wasn't going to rain on her parade today.

The receptionist took her time putting on a stylish pair of reading glasses and perusing her computer screen. "Ah, yes, you're to go right up." She gave Patrice the office number and pointed in the direction of the bank of elevators. "Hurry, you're going to be late in five minutes."

"Thank you," said Patrice, rolling her eyes when her back was to the woman.

Power trips were so ugly.

A few minutes later, she walked into the reception area of Mark Greenberg's office and had to face another receptionist. This one was male, African-American and perfectly turned out in a dark blue suit and tie. There was no one else in the office. He rose when he saw her and grinned broadly. "Wow, Ms. Sutton, it's really you, in the flesh!" His outburst must have been unintentional because he suddenly looked stricken. "Sorry," he said, chagrined.

Patrice liked him immediately.

She offered him her hand in greeting. He took it and held it in both of his as he smiled at her. "I loved you in *Amsterdam Avenue*."

Patrice smiled at the mention of her now-canceled sitcom. She had portrayed—what else—an out-of-work actress, in the well-received situation comedy. The show had been called *Amsterdam Avenue* because of the prevalence of creative people like actors, dancers and singers living in that part of Manhattan.

"You're a Kym fan, huh?" she said. "Thanks, I had a lot of fun on that show."

"I couldn't wait to see what kind of trouble Kym would get into from week to week," he said. "Oh, I've seen your movies, too."

"That was you?" Patrice joked. "I hear they sold about two tickets. You must have taken a date with you."

He laughed uproariously. He laughed so loudly that Mark Greenberg came out of his office to see what all the fuss was about.

"Patrice, you're here," he exclaimed upon seeing her. "T.K. and I have been waiting for you." He laughed shortly when he saw that his assistant still had a grip on Patrice's hand. "Calvin, if you'll let go of Ms. Sutton, we'll get the meeting started."

Calvin looked embarrassed and abruptly let go of her. "I'm sorry, Ms. Sutton."

Patrice smiled at him. "It's been a pleasure chatting with you, Calvin."

He followed them to the door of Mark's office. "Can I get you anything? Coffee, tea, bottled water, a muffin? I can go out and get you something if we don't have it."

"No, thank you. I'm fine," said Patrice as Mark grabbed her by the arm and gently pulled her inside his office, whereupon he firmly, if not rudely, shut the door in Calvin's face.

"I apologize for that," he said softly as they walked

into his spacious office. "Calvin is usually not as effusive when he meets celebrities. I suppose he's a really big fan of yours. I should have known something was up when he arrived at work this morning looking like a *GQ* model. We're usually more casual around here."

He was wearing jeans and a button-down shirt with a pair of expensive athletic shoes—the same sort of clothing he'd been wearing when Patrice had first met him a few weeks ago at her audition. At that meeting, the casting director had been the primary interviewer. Mark had simply observed.

"No need," Patrice graciously said, discreetly looking around for T.K. "He's sweet."

A tall, well-built man in jeans, a polo shirt and athletic shoes stood at the panoramic picture window, his back to them. Mark cleared his throat. "T.K., I'd like you to meet Patrice Sutton."

T.K. turned around. He and Patrice walked toward one another, meeting in the center of the room. They shook hands. His big hand swallowed hers. His palm was warm and dry and his skin was kind of rough. Strangely, the roughness of his hand impressed her. Usually, actors' hands were as soft as hers. It wasn't as if they worked as laborers or ranchers, the job she traditionally associated with "real" men.

"Good to meet you, Patrice," T.K. said, smiling down at her. He was six-four to her five-seven.

Patrice smiled back at him. Her throat suddenly felt dry. She cleared it. "Good to meet you, too, T.K.," she softly said. All she was thinking at that moment was *Blanca was wrong. Oh, God, I'm holding T. K. McKenna's hand!*

She released his hand. After releasing *his* hand, she didn't seem to know what to do with *hers*. She tugged her shoulder bag closer to her side and looked around for Mark, who had become her safe harbor in a stormy sea. She didn't know why being in T. K. McKenna's presence made her nervous. She'd met some of the most successful actors in the business, luminaries who were considered legends, and she had managed to maintain her dignity.

She had known he was magnificent to behold. She had seen practically all of his 30 films. However, the physical impact of seeing him in person magnified his sex appeal tenfold. For one thing, he smelled wonderful. She just wanted to go to him, bury her nose in his muscular chest and stay there awhile. Also, his burnished honey skin was beautiful; that was the only word for it. Usually she preferred men with rich dark-chocolate skin, but even though his wasn't very dark, it was very appealing. She itched to touch him, rub his bald head.

T.K., who was used to making people nervous, immediately recognized that Patrice was a bit flustered. He casually put a bit of distance between them, going again to stand near the window, talking the whole time. "Mark tells me you ride."

Mark came and took Patrice by the elbow and directed her to one of the plush leather armchairs in front of his desk. "Make yourself comfortable."

He went and sat behind his desk. T.K. remained standing. From across the room, his magnetic gaze held hers.

"I grew up on a ranch in New Mexico," Patrice said, her voice stronger now.

He looked impressed. His brown eyes held an amused glint. "No kidding, a working ranch?"

"Yes, with cattle and horses and everything," Patrice told him with a shy smile.

He couldn't help noticing that some of the tension had gone out of her expression. She apparently loved talking about the ranch.

"Your folks still run it?" he asked.

"Suttons have been running it since the late 1800s," Patrice said proudly.

T.K. went and pulled another of the leather chairs close to hers and sat down. He leaned toward her. "That's fascinating. Have you read the script yet?" He wasn't sure whether or not she'd been provided with a script. Sometimes the casting director gave the actor only part of it to read during the audition.

Patrice glanced at Mark. Before she had left after auditioning for the casting director, he had given her the script. At the time, Patrice had thought it odd that one of the producers would discreetly give her a script, but now she understood that Mark had seen something in her that he had liked that day. That's why he had given it to her.

She smiled at Mark. "Mark gave me a copy. It's a wonderful story."

"Did you know it's loosely based on the life and times of a real black lawman?"

She did. She had researched Frontier Marshal Bass Reeves after reading the script.

"I found a couple of books online about him," she told him. She smiled at T.K. "You look kind of like him. However, he was only six-two, and he had a handlebar mustache."

T.K. looked over at Mark and grinned. "She's done her homework."

"What made you want to tell the story of Bass Reeves?" she asked both of them.

Mark deferred to T.K. T.K. leaned back in his chair before beginning, thinking he was crowding Patrice and she might get skittish again if he didn't back off a little. He found himself naturally drawn to the attractive actress. She had the kind of rich brown skin with red undertones that he loved. Her sooty black hair was healthy-looking and shone like a raven's wing. Her dark, wide-spaced eyes were beautiful. He tried not to look at those full red lips because he kept getting an image of them kissing whenever he did. He didn't know if the fact that she had grown up on a ranch made him see her as a natural beauty or if it was simply that she appeared so fresh to him. She fairly glowed, and unlike some actresses who knew their effect on males, she appeared quite unaware of her sex appeal. If she were aware, she would be looking him straight in the eyes with a confident expression in her own. She found it difficult looking into his eyes for any length of time, and she was blushing like crazy. He decided that Patrice Sutton was a very sweet, unaffected girl. He hoped she stayed that way.

"It's a piece of the American West that has been sorely neglected," he said of wanting to tell Bass Reeves's story. "We've had movies about Wyatt Earp, 'Wild Bill' Hickok, but nothing about Reeves, who was just as big a legend as those men. He was good with a gun. He tracked down and arrested countless outlaws and killed fourteen of them in fair gunfights."

"Where does the character I read for, Bella Donna, come in? Was she a real person, too?"

"I'm afraid not," T.K. told her. "Not much was written about his relationship with women."

"The scriptwriter made her up at our request," Mark told her. "We thought the lawman should have a noble love."

"So the writer made her a prostitute?" said Patrice incredulously. She couldn't help it. If Bella Donna was a fictional character, the writer could have made her a schoolteacher.

"Prostitutes were prevalent in those days," T.K. said unapologetically. "Because women were so scarce in some areas, oftentimes those were the only kind of women a man saw for years. Think of the lack of opportunities women had back then. Bella Donna might be a prostitute, but she's also loving and extremely tough. She's a worthy mate for the marshal."

"Aren't you afraid of what the NAACP is going to say about your film? It's wonderful to remind moviegoers of a great man in history, a great black man, but to pair him with a prostitute? Some people are going to be upset about that."

T.K. smiled. "A film that doesn't cause controversy doesn't cause a stir in the minds of moviegoers. It'll be good for box-office receipts."

Patrice nodded in agreement. He was a shrewd businessman as well as a fine actor. "All right, I understand your reasoning."

"Does that mean you want to work with us?" T.K. asked hopefully.

Patrice's stomach muscles tightened in panic. Was he actually offering her the role of a lifetime? She looked into his eyes. T.K. smiled. "Sounds tempting," she said, appearing perfectly calm when she was a quivering bowl of jelly inside. "Let me sleep on it and get back to you tomorrow."

Blanca had instructed her to never accept a first offer. "You don't want to appear desperate, chica," was Blanca's advice.

"Fair enough," said T.K. He got to his feet. Mark rose, too. Patrice didn't move for a moment. The shock of being offered the role had rendered her legs momentarily weak.

She took a deep breath and got to her feet. Offering

T.K. her hand, she said, "My sister is going to scream in my ear when I tell her I met you. She adores you."

T.K. took her hand and covered it with his other one. "Tell her it was I who was impressed with her sister."

Patrice's heartbeat doubled when he said that even though she knew he was just being nice. She supposed a man like T. K. McKenna had had plenty of practice charming women. Of course, a star of his stature didn't have to put forth much effort to entice women. They were probably throwing themselves at him on a daily basis.

"She's family," Patrice joked. "She'll never believe it."

T.K. laughed. Yes, he was well aware of how truly unimpressed family members could be about your success as an actor. To millions of people, you were an idol. But to your family, you were just the boy who slept with a teddy bear until you were nine.

Family knew where all your skeletons were buried. Heck, they'd helped you bury them.

The three of them walked to the door.

"Thanks for coming, Patrice," Mark said, smiling warmly. "I hope you decide to sign on. We're not that bad to work with. As one of the producers, you'll rarely see me on the set, and T.K. is reportedly now a dream to work with since I convinced him to quit doing the Tarzan yell every time he got a scene right. That was *very* unsettling."

"It was also bad for the voice," T.K. said, playing along.

Patrice laughed. "You guys are crazy." She reached into her bag and retrieved her cell phone.

"Uh-oh," said Mark. "We're so boring she's going to make a phone call right in the middle of a conversation."

"I'm phoning for a cab," she explained. "Hopefully it'll get here not too long after I get downstairs."

"A cab?" said T.K. "You don't drive?"

"Of course I drive," Patrice explained. "However, my car is in Albuquerque." She told them how her car happened to be in New Mexico while she was in California.

"Since you went to so much trouble to be here today, the least I can do is give you a lift home," T.K. gallantly offered.

"That's very nice of you, but I don't want you to go out of your way," Patrice said hurriedly. Here she was about to get out of his presence so that her heart rate could return to some semblance of normal, and he was suggesting they spend *more* time together?

"How do you know it's out of my way?" T.K. asked reasonably. "I don't even know where you live." He peered down at her with a concerned expression.

"Beverly Hills," Patrice told him. "Well, not in one of the pricier neighborhoods. I live in a nice bungalow south of Santa Monica Boulevard."

"That's not out of my way," T.K. insisted.

"All right, if you're sure," Patrice said reluctantly.

They were in the outer office now. Calvin looked

expectantly at Patrice. She smiled at him. "Goodbye, Calvin. It was nice meeting you."

Beaming with pleasure, he quickly crossed the room and shook her hand again. "It was my pleasure, Ms. Sutton. Please come again soon."

Mark's hand was on the small of Patrice's back, ushering her from the outer office and into T.K.'s capable hands. She wondered if Mark was hoping T.K. would use his considerable charm on the ride to Beverly Hills to persuade her to go ahead and sign on with them. She had felt their disappointment when she had told them she needed time to think.

She and T.K. were alone on the elevator ride downstairs. "Where's your entourage?" she asked, a teasing glint in her eyes.

"I don't have one," T.K. said, smiling at her. "Where's yours?"

"You're looking at her," joked Patrice.

He gave her an intimate perusal, his eyes sweeping over her face. It felt like a caress to her, and she blushed. She also lowered her eyes.

T.K. laughed softly. "You're not still nervous around me, are you?"

She looked up. "Who said I was nervous around you?"

"I can usually tell when I make someone nervous," said T.K., the smile never leaving his face. "You look very pretty when you blush."

Patrice started to ask him how he knew she was

blushing when, to her knowledge, her cheeks didn't change color when she felt embarrassed. However, the elevator doors opened onto the lobby, and there were several people waiting to get on.

A small commotion ensued when T.K. was recognized, and soon he was being asked to sign his name on everything from a laptop to a woman's smooth, flat belly. Patrice tried not to laugh. It was amazing how shame flew out the window when T. K. McKenna showed up in a lobby of unsuspecting females. T.K. declined to sign the woman's belly but complimented her on its tone. "You must work out a lot," he said kindly.

"Every day," the woman said, producing a piece of paper from her portfolio for T.K. to sign.

After that, T.K. made his apologies, and taking Patrice by the hand, they hurried from the building.

"You can't go anywhere without that happening, can you?" Patrice asked as they racewalked across the street to the parking garage where T.K. had left his SUV.

"It's not so bad," he said nonchalantly. "It's not a high price to pay for fame and fortune. After all, they're the ones who go to see my movies. I owe them a certain amount of consideration. But I know where to draw the line. I don't let the fame control my actions."

Patrice smiled up at him. The sunlight made his brown eyes appear honey-colored.

She liked his attitude. It's how she looked at celebrity, too. She didn't mind meeting the fans; in fact, she loved it. However, there were times when she fiercely guarded her privacy. For example, when she was being interviewed, reporters were free to try to pick her apart, but her family was a forbidden subject.

T.K. still held her hand as they crossed the street. He liked holding her hand. He didn't know what that meant at this point except that she was very pleasant to be around. He was completely comfortable in her presence, even if he still made her a little nervous.

At the late-model Range Rover, he unlocked the doors and handed Patrice in. When he was behind the wheel and had relocked the doors, he turned to her and asked, "What are you doing for lunch?"

"Lunch?" asked Patrice, sounding startled by his question.

He laughed softly. "Yes, the meal that comes a few hours after breakfast, which I skipped this morning except for a cup of coffee and a swallow of orange juice. Have you been to The Grill? They make great food, really fresh. Good fish if you're not a red-meat eater. Vegetarian dishes, too."

"No, I've never been there," Patrice told him. She breathed deeply and slowly released her breath. "Are you sure you don't have to be anywhere else?"

"Nah, I'm on vacation until we start filming." He started the SUV, and soon they were turning onto the street and heading toward the San Diego Freeway where he would exit onto Santa Monica Boulevard. From there, it was only three miles to Beverly Hills.

"I'm sorry," he said suddenly as he wound his way

through traffic. "I didn't even ask if you were free. If you have plans for the afternoon, I can take you directly home."

"I'm free," Patrice assured him. She had decided to go with the flow.

He turned and smiled at her before returning his attention to the road. "Good."

Patrice relaxed against the car's seat. "You said your parents live in Beverly Hills?"

He must have been fond of his parents because his eyes lit up at the mention of them. "Yes, I finally talked them into moving here about five years ago. We're from Brooklyn.

"My parents have deep roots there. Both were born there. Both were teachers for nearly thirty years. Most of their friends and family still live in Brooklyn."

"What did you say to convince them to move here?" she asked, very curious. She couldn't imagine her parents living in Beverly Hills. It would be a worse situation than that old sitcom *The Beverly Hillbillies*. Her folks were ranchers, through and through.

"I told them that I didn't care when the desire to go back to Brooklyn hit them. I would make sure they got on the next plane flying in that direction," he said with a laugh.

"You're a good son," Patrice complimented him.

"I try to be," T.K. said sincerely.

Chapter 3

At The Grill on the Alley, commonly called The Grill,
T.K. gave his key to the valet and then helped Patrice
out of the car. He enjoyed the sight of her long, shapely
legs but was careful not to ogle. Patrice noticed anyway
and felt a tingle of excitement.

Inside, they were immediately shown to a secluded
table in the back of the packed dining room. T.K. didn't
let the maître d' have the pleasure of pulling Patrice's
chair out for her. He did it himself and then sat down
across from her.

The maître d' snapped his fingers at a passing waiter.
"See to Mr. McKenna at once."

He smiled at T.K. and Patrice in turn. "Please call on
me if I can be of any further service."

When he had gone, T.K. laughed softly. "Every time

I see him I'm reminded of the butler in that remake of *Mr. Deeds Goes to Town.*"

"He does look like John Turturro. He's one of my favorite actors," Patrice said enthusiastically. "In everything I've ever seen him in, he's done a good job."

T.K. nodded in agreement. "He's a fine character actor." He looked at her intently. "What did you think of the remake?"

"Adam Sandler makes me laugh, and it had some touching moments, but to be honest, I don't believe any remake can compare with the Frank Capra original. The script's fabulous, and Gary Cooper is wonderful as *Mr. Deeds.* Good try to Adam Sandler, though."

T.K. smiled at her assessment. He liked the original a lot better than the remake, too.

"You like Capra, huh?"

"*It's a Wonderful Life, You Can't Take it With You,* and *Mr. Deeds Goes to Town* are my favorite Capra films," she told him, her eyes shining with excitement. "The scripts were excellent, and the leads and supporting casts were, too. Plus, I liked the dignity Capra imbued his black characters with. Yes, they were servants, but they were treated with respect and got actual lines to say instead of standing around rolling their eyes and grinning."

"You have a problem with the way blacks have been portrayed in films?" T.K. was curious. He wanted to know if she had a fire in her belly to see her people portrayed accurately on film, as he had.

The waiter arrived and introduced himself. They promptly ordered and sent him on his way, eager to continue their conversation.

"You were saying," T.K. prompted Patrice after the waiter had gone.

"What black actor wouldn't have a problem with the way we've been portrayed by some filmmakers?" she asked. "But I'm not going the route of blaming the performers of the past. They had to play the buffoon in order to put food on the table. I respect them because they survived during a very unpleasant time for blacks."

T.K. smiled at the way she punctuated her words with her hands. Fleetingly, she reminded him of Shiva, the many-armed Hindu goddess. He didn't know where that thought came from. She stimulated his mind, he supposed.

"What about black filmmakers today?" he asked. "Do you think they're doing everything they can do to bring accurate depictions of blacks to the silver screen?"

Patrice pursed her lips and squinted at him. "Don't get me started on that subject. My actor friends say my opinions are unusual to say the least."

"Go ahead and shock me," he coaxed. "This goes no farther than this table."

"All right," she said, leaning toward him. "I won't name names because you already know them anyway. But I don't think a certain director should be throwing stones at another one simply because they make different types of films. So what if the newcomer's films are sometimes over-the-top and melodramatic? Hollywood has been producing melodramatic films for ages. One of the most beloved films by black folks, *Imitation of Life,* is extremely melodramatic. But that doesn't mean we don't watch it, raptly, whenever it comes on Turner Classic Movies."

T.K. laughed. "You're right. The scene where the daughter barely makes it to her mother's funeral on time and makes a spectacle of herself is a seminal scene. And I believe, to this day, that Juanita Moore should have won the Oscar for her role."

"She was robbed," Patrice agreed heartily. "I can't watch her final scenes without crying."

"Okay," T.K. said, "we agree that the way blacks were depicted in the past was largely not their fault. And Tyler Perry is definitely doing something right."

"We said no names," Patrice reminded him, pretending to be scandalized that he would name one of the parties they were discussing.

"No harm in acknowledging someone who's making a difference for black actors in the industry. Critics might not get him, but I assure you out-of-work actors love him."

"T.K.!" exclaimed a booming male voice as a tall, slender black man approached their table. Patrice peered up—and up—at Los Angeles Lakers forward Farrell

Faison. Farrell was six-seven. T.K. stood up and shook his hand. "Hello, Farrell, how are you, man?"

"Cool, cool," said Farrell. He looked at Patrice with interest. Patrice smiled up at him. She admired his skill on the court. When she was in town, she tried to go to all the team's home games. It was the off-season now.

"Aren't you going to introduce me?" he asked T.K.

"Why don't you sit down first," T.K. joked. "I'm getting a crick in my neck from having to look up."

Farrell laughed and took the seat closest to Patrice's. He didn't even glance in T.K.'s direction anymore, just looked at Patrice with a smile on his face.

"Farrell, I'd like you to meet—" T.K. said.

"Ms. Patrice Sutton," Farrell said with a contented sigh. "I just saw you in *She Fell*. Wow, not only was the science-fiction story line kickin', but you were awesome as Victoria." He shook his head as if he were amazed that he was sitting across from the warrior-woman Victoria. "How long did it take you to get in shape for that role?"

"Six months of grueling aerobics and weight-lifting," Patrice told him, happy to meet someone who had enjoyed *She Fell*. It was the film she was proudest of. A friend who was a writer had specifically written the character of Victoria for her. In the story, Victoria was sent through a man-made black hole to a warlike planet by her evil but brilliant physicist husband who got rid of all his enemies by sending them God-knows-where via the black hole. He had drugged and sent Victoria through because she was going to divorce him for infidelity. The film follows Victoria as she rises in power as a warrior. In the end, she returns to Earth and exacts revenge on her husband.

"Who's your trainer?" Farrell asked.

"Jose Baltodano," Patrice happily supplied. She was always willing to refer anyone who wanted to get into shape to her friend.

T.K. cleared his throat and playfully glared at Farrell. "Let me get this straight, you came over here to monopolize my date's time?"

Farrell grinned at him. "Turnabout is fair play, my brother."

Patrice smiled at that. T.K. had obviously flirted with Farrell's dates in the past. Then it hit her: T.K. had referred to her as his date. She looked into his eyes. He winked at her.

"I have to protest, *my brother*," he said to Farrell. "I just met Patrice myself. You could have at least given me a twenty-four-hour head start before you began poaching on my territory."

Patrice laughed and rose. "I'll let you fellas figure out the proper poaching etiquette while I visit the ladies' room. Excuse me."

She overheard Farrell say, "She's too young for you, old man. She'll give you a heart attack."

"I'm willing to risk it," said T.K.

Smiling, Patrice kept walking.

In the ladies' room, a feminine room replete with a settee, she sat down and dialed Blanca's number.

Blanca answered right away. "Well, how'd it go?" she asked breathlessly.

"It went very well," Patrice said as she crossed her legs and got comfortable on the plush covered settee. "They want me."

"I knew it!" cried Blanca, sounding happy and calculating all at once. "You didn't accept, though?"

"No, I told them I would let them know tomorrow."

"Why do you keep saying *they* and *them?*" asked Blanca curiously.

"Because T.K. sat in on the meeting, too," said Patrice, calmly dropping the bomb and waiting for the explosion.

"What?" yelled Blanca. "Mark must have really liked you. This is fantastic. I don't know if I'll be able to wait until tomorrow for you to give them a yes."

"Are you saying you're going to break your cardinal rule?"

"Rules are made to be broken," said Blanca. She laughed softly. "Patty, do you know what this means? Forget about working for two years on the sitcom and those really fine movies you've done that brought you a little bit of fame. They were dues you had to pay to get here. You've arrived!"

Patrice was laughing, too. "It feels good to be wanted."

Blanca took a deep breath. "Where are you now? I

promised a celebration, remember? Where do you want to go tonight? Anywhere you want to go, it's my treat."

"I hate to be a party pooper, but I'd prefer to spend a quiet evening at home. Thanks for the offer though. I'm having lunch with T.K. right now," Patrice told her agent. She explained about having to phone a taxi and T.K.'s offer of a lift.

"His parents raised him right," Blanca said of T.K.'s being a gentleman. "Okay, I'll tell you what. Before you two part, assure him that you'll be delighted to work with him, and I'll give Mark a call about the contract."

"Will do," Patrice promised.

"Congratulations," said Blanca sincerely. "I'm really proud of you."

"Thanks, Blanca."

After hanging up, Patrice rose to check her makeup in the wide mirror over the double sinks. A woman walked in and hurried to a stall.

Seeing nothing wrong with her face, she left the bathroom. When she got within sight of her table, she saw that Farrell had left.

T.K. got up and pulled her chair out. "Farrell remembered a previous engagement."

Patrice met his eyes. His look was enigmatic. She wished she could have heard their conversation in her absence. "Too bad," she said. "I'd never met him before. He seems like a nice guy."

"He is," T.K. assured her.

He looked up, spotted their waiter and gestured to

him. "The waiter wanted to serve our meals while you were gone, but I told him to keep them warm until you got back."

"That was considerate of you."

"I'm a considerate guy."

Patrice let her gaze roam over his face, admiring the strong, masculine shape of his jaw, the fullness of his lips. He smiled the whole while as though he were perfectly fine with her lusting after him with her eyes.

No harm in looking, Patrice thought. The harm comes in acting on your desires. She didn't plan to do that. She did not become romantically involved with actors she worked with. Work was work, and play was play.

Rumor had it that T.K. didn't share her opinion on the subject. He had been linked with a few women while they were working on a film together. He didn't make it a habit like some actors she knew, but the fact that none of those relationships had worked out concerned her. At thirty-six, he had never been married. He could be gay. Nah, she immediately dismissed that. Back in the day it had been possible for Hollywood to hide the fact that some of its leading men—and women—were gay, but these days the tabloids uncovered anyone who was in the closet. She hated tabloid journalism, if you could call it journalism.

She realized they had been looking into each other's eyes the past five minutes without saying a word. She laughed. "I often thought that you were mesmerizing on the big screen, but I never suspected you might be in person."

T.K. smiled. "Does that mean you'll be my Bella Donna?"

"I'll be Bass Reeves's Bella Donna," Patrice corrected him with a wry smile.

T.K. took her hand in his and kissed her knuckles. The feel of his warm mouth on her skin made her sigh involuntarily. He raised his head and looked her in the eyes. "Same difference," he said. "Lucky for me, it'll be Bass Reeves kissing you but my lips doing the deed."

"Just so you both know where *not* to put your hands," joked Patrice. T.K. laughed.

The waiter arrived at that moment and served their meals.

Patrice wound up spending a quiet night at home. After phoning family and friends to tell them of her good fortune, she reread the script to *Bass Reeves, Lawman.* Blanca phoned to say she'd spoken with Mark Greenberg and that the lawyers were working on the contract. He promised that it would be in Blanca's hands in a matter of days.

Patrice was curled up on the sofa in the living room of her modest bungalow. She was wearing shorts and a tank top because it was warm tonight. The house had air-conditioning but she rarely turned it on unless the temperature rose to the nineties. She liked to sleep with her windows open. It was something she might not do if she lived in greater Los Angeles, but the Beverly Hills police boasted that they could be at your door within a minute of being summoned. She had not had the opportunity to test that boast.

As she read, she found herself chuckling from time to time. The Western was an action/adventure, but it had funny moments, especially the exchanges between Bella and Bass who seemed to love arguing as much as they did making love.

When she got to the love scene, she let out a groan. It was *hot*. She and T.K. would have to be practically naked. Of course, key parts of their bodies would be concealed from the eyes of those present on the set during the filming of it. But she knew that to the audience it would appear that she and T.K. had been completely nude during the filming. She had never done a nude scene. She panicked. What would her parents think? What would the people at the church she'd gone to when she was growing up say? Her family still attended that church!

She got up, fanning herself with the script. How could she have missed that scene when she had read the script before? She blamed it on her habit of skimming over the directions in the script in favor of her character's dialogue. There was no dialogue in the love scene. There was only direction: where T.K. would put his hands; where, when and how she was to moan as if in ecstasy.

She looked over at the clock on the mantel above the fireplace. It was 9:13 p.m. Blanca didn't usually go to bed this early. Blanca had made a copy of the script for her personal use. She grabbed her cell phone from the coffee table and dialed her number.

As soon as Blanca answered, she cried, "Did you read the love scene?"

"Fabulous, isn't it?" Blanca said sleepily. "I haven't read anything that perfectly erotic in a long time. It's a mature scene with two people who truly love each other. It's tender because it's goodbye for them, even though neither of them is aware of it. Bella gets killed the next day. It's the kind of scene people are going to be talking about for a long time, especially women. Bella directs him. She shows him how to love her like she wants to be loved, and Bass is more than willing to oblige. I tell you, women are going to fast-forward to that scene when it comes out on DVD again and again and live vicariously through you."

"I don't know if I want them to live vicariously through me!"

"Don't tell me you're getting cold feet," said Blanca with an indulgent laugh. "Do you know how many actresses would kill you to replace you in that scene?"

"I'm sure there would be quite a few," Patrice admitted. "I'm still leery about showing so much skin."

"No, you're nervous about portraying a black woman as a sexual being," Blanca lightly accused, her tone still humorous. "Patty, I understand your reticence, but think of the portrayals of black women in Oscar-winning roles. You've got a maid, a psychic who was the comic relief and a tortured soul who has an affair with the white man who was one of the guards on duty when her husband was executed. There is no example of a black woman loving a black man the way he should be loved. Sleep on that, and call me tomorrow. I'm your friend as well as your agent. If you really don't want to do the role, then I'll start looking for something better for you."

Patrice sat down hard on the couch. Blanca was right. There was so much negativity out there where black men and women were concerned. Moviegoers needed more positive examples of black men loving black women. Sex was a normal, healthy part of being in love with someone. The manner in which it was expressed in the script was not salacious or pornographic.

She took a deep breath. "I don't have to sleep on it. I want to do it. I just panicked for a moment, there. Sorry to wake you."

"I wasn't asleep," Blanca denied.

"Blanca, I've been calling you and waking you up for a few years now. I know how you sound when you first wake up."

Blanca laughed. "All right, you got me. Good night, chica."

"Good night," Patrice said softly, feeling a lot better about the script. She hung up the phone, picked up the script, sat down and continued reading. Bella was killed the next day. Good death scene, Patrice thought. She died bravely. Later in the script, Bass avenged Bella's murder.

Tears were in Patrice's eyes when she finished reading.

She wondered what T.K. was doing at that moment. Had his flirting been genuine? Or had he done it just because he knew women expected him to be charming and attentive when they were with him?

Chapter 4

That night, T.K. was running on the beach near his house in Malibu. He liked running at night when the world around him was quieter. He liked running on the beach because of the extra resistance the damp sand provided. He got a better workout. An added bonus was that the sound of the ocean soothed him.

He was wearing a sleeveless T-shirt, shorts and running shoes. Much of the heat of the day had dissipated, but it was still a temperate seventy-five degrees out. Sam, his golden retriever, sneezed next to him, and T.K. laughed. "What's the matter, boy, am I kicking up too much sand for you?"

Sam, of course, didn't answer but happily ran on beside his human. They were only a half mile from the house. T.K. would be sure to spoil him a little tonight—maybe give him one of those doggy ice-cream treats he loved so much.

Now that Malcolm was gone, Sam was his only housemate. When he was alive Malcolm had loved to care for Sam. Sometimes T.K. would walk into the living room and find man and dog sitting in front of the TV watching some inane comedy, Malcolm laughing uproariously and Sam smiling. Occasionally, when he would go into the living room now, he would expect to find Malcolm there. He supposed it would take his mind a while to accept that his brother was gone forever.

At the house, he and Sam jogged up the back steps of the house that led from the beach. He doffed his shoes on the balcony. He didn't want to track sand into the house. Sam patiently stood while he wiped him off with an old towel he kept on the balcony for that purpose. They entered the house through the kitchen entrance.

He got a bottle of water from the fridge and poured some in Sam's dish for him and drank the rest. Then he began the trek upstairs. Although the house was big at five thousand square feet, it wasn't ostentatious. He preferred clean lines, and possessions weren't that important to him. The furnishings were expensive only because he thought you got what you paid for. He was a big man, and the last thing he wanted to worry about was his bed collapsing under him because it was cheaply made. He was sensible in that way.

Sam followed him all the way to his bedroom. At the door, he turned to the dog and said, "I'll be down in a few minutes. I want to shower, and then I'll give you a good brushing and a treat for being such a trouper tonight."

Sam peered up at him as though he understood him perfectly, whined, turned around and padded back downstairs.

T.K. walked over to the nightstand next to the side of the bed where he slept and pressed the message button on the answering machine. His mother had phoned while he was out. "Your father and I are going to New York for the weekend and will be leaving Aisha alone in the house. If you would call her to check on her once or twice while we're gone, we would appreciate it."

T.K. dreaded doing that. Aisha turned into a sultry vixen when she spoke with him over the phone. It was as if she lost the ability to speak normally. Why she thought he wanted to hear his brother's girlfriend cooing in his ear, he could not imagine. Trying to sound sexy wasn't going to make him warm up to her. He kept his distance because whenever she looked at him there was a hungry, predatory expression in her eyes.

He hated to put a pregnant woman in her place, but if it continued he was going to have to bluntly do so.

The next message was from Mark. "I just got off the phone with Blanca Mendes, Patrice's agent. That's one formidable lady. She's sensible too, though. They didn't ask for any outrageous perks, but she made sure to protect her client's rights. Patrice will be able to start in late August when we begin filming. She has another film that begins rolling in March, though, so we need to be finished with her scenes before then. I don't anticipate running over schedule, but you never can anticipate the elements, and you're going to be in the Badlands. Have a good night."

T.K. had been pulling off his clothes as he listened. Naked, he strode into the bathroom and turned on the water in the shower. Patrice Sutton. He tried not to think too much about her. She was so sweet. When he closed his eyes and inhaled deeply, he imagined he could still smell the enticing scent of her.

It was too soon after his breakup with Edina to consider allowing another woman to get close to him. He knew most people expected the male in a relationship to have a roving eye, but in theirs it had been Edina who had cheated on him—repeatedly. Plus, she had had the gall to blame him. His schedule, she accused, didn't allow them enough time to grow as a couple. What she meant was he wasn't there every night to satisfy her sexual needs. Well, she hadn't been with him every night to satisfy his needs either, but he hadn't gone out and found some willing substitute for her. To be truthful with himself, he was more embarrassed than heartbroken because he had suspected for some time now that Edina, who was an actress, was with him only to further her career. He wasn't conceited enough, even though he was admittedly a fine example of a black male, to believe that he could be the complete answer to a woman's prayers. No man was that perfect. A woman had to be happy with her life without a man in it before she could find happiness with a man. She needed to know what she wanted out of life and be willing to sacrifice for it. That was Edina's problem. She wanted instant gratification. She wasn't willing to work for happiness and didn't care who she hurt in her efforts to coast through life.

When he was feeling particularly depressed he would ask himself if he had been a better lover whether she would have cheated. Then he would remind himself that he was never a selfish lover. When they made love, he had given her his full attention. Now he knew how women felt when men cheated on them: dignity and self-worth take a beating. The truth was cheaters will stray no matter how well their significant others perform in bed. They're selfish and greedy, always looking for the next thrill.

He wasn't about the next thrill any longer. In this fake world in which he made a living, there were too many people who were looking for a thrill, ready to provide one or had enjoyed one too many and had ended up dead, broke or both.

He had been working as an actor for nearly eighteen years—half his life. He'd been through his stupid stage during which he'd believed the hype about how talented he was and gladly accepted the hangers-on, the groupies and all the false adulation that went with it. These days, he spurned insincere people.

Of course, because the insincere usually outnumbered the sincere, he spent a lot of time alone, which was fine with him.

Patrice Sutton, though, was worth pondering. He smiled when he remembered sparring with Farrell over her. Why had he done that if he truly was not ready to consider letting another woman into his life? Farrell had genuinely been interested in asking Patrice out, but while Patrice was in the ladies' room T.K. effectively convinced the young rival for her affections that she was off-limits. Perhaps that hadn't been fair to Patrice. She should have had the opportunity to either accept Farrell's attentions or turn them down. To his credit, T.K. was probably saving her from a broken heart because Farrell, at twenty-five, was a long way from abandoning the player's lifestyle. Women were constantly throwing themselves at him. And unlike T.K., who had learned to turn them down, Farrell was still flattered by the attention and willing to take advantage of the eager women.

After a quick shower, he dried off and put on his robe. Stepping into a pair of black leather slippers, he went downstairs.

Sam was waiting for him at the bottom, intelligent eyes smiling. He apparently hadn't forgotten the earlier promise of a treat.

"Yeah, yeah," said T.K. with a laugh. "You earned your ice cream tonight."

Sam turned and trotted ahead of him to the kitchen. T.K. wondered what the tabloids would make of one of the most popular movie stars in the world spending a Friday night with a dog. They wouldn't call him a stud then.

* * *

Her cell phone ringing woke Patrice Saturday morning. She gave the display a bleary-eyed stare. Then she pressed Talk. "Hey, Patrick, what's up?"

Her younger brother by two years laughed. "You sound drunk. I know you don't drink that much so I must have woken you."

"Excellent deduction, Professor Sutton," said Patrice as she sat up in bed.

"I've got my doctorate, but it'll be a long time before I'm tenured," said Patrick, still chuckling. "I hear you're going to be cavorting with T. K. McKenna in a Western. It's about time they made another good Western with black lead actors."

"I know. Isn't it pitiful? The last watchable one was *Posse* with Mario Van Peebles," Patrice enthusiastically agreed.

"Didn't Will Smith make a Western?" Patrick asked.

"Yes, he did," Patrice said. "I'll leave it at that."

Patrick laughed. "It wasn't that bad. Anyway, big sis, congratulations, I'm proud of you. Now, don't go falling in love with T. K. McKenna. Nina says he's never been down the aisle. She says he's either a hard-core bachelor or gay. Either way, you'll wind up getting your heart broken."

Patrice wondered when her sister-in-law, who was a full-time law student, had time to read the tabloids. "He's not gay."

"I didn't think he was," said her brother with a bit of

relief in his tone. There was a muffled exchange in the background, and then Nina's somewhat squeaky voice came over the line. "Hey, Patty. What's up?"

"Hi, Nina," Patrice said with real pleasure. She liked her sister-in-law. She had a zest for life. She kept her usually shy, bookish brother happily on his toes trying to keep up with her.

"I know you couldn't care less, but Edina Edwards was on a late-night talk show a few nights ago talking about her engagement to some music mogul. I can't recall his name. Anyway, the host looked surprised and said he didn't know she had broken up with T.K. You could tell he said it just to provoke her. They broke up about four months ago. He was just needling her for getting engaged so soon after it was reported that she'd cheated on T.K. and that's why they'd broken up. He got his money's worth, too, because she got up and stormed off the set. You didn't hear about it? It's all over the Net and the entertainment news shows!"

"Poor T.K.," said Patrice. She knew that T.K. and Edina Edwards had ended their relationship but none of the particulars. She only knew that they had been a couple for over two years. They had met while doing a film together.

She didn't feel inclined to gossip about him now, especially after meeting him and liking him as a person. He must be hurting after the way Edina treated him, she thought sympathetically. And now she's gotten engaged to someone else after only four months—possibly to the man she cheated on him with.

"Yeah, poor guy," Nina said. "But yay for you, sis, because I don't agree with my husband, who thinks you should try *not* to fall for him. He's available, and he's fair game. I say, go for it!"

Patrice laughed. "Please, Nina, don't go putting those thoughts in my head. The man is scrumptious up close and personal. I'm going to have a hard enough time working with him day in and day out without constantly having images of him naked in my mind!"

Nina laughed heartily. When she was over her laughing fit, she said seriously, "I know you were saying that to humor me. You're so levelheaded, Patty. Sometimes I wish you would live it up and break your rules for a change." She sighed. "I'm putting my money on T.K. If anybody can make you loosen up, he can."

Patrice took that as a challenge—not that she thought for one minute that T.K. had any notion whatsoever of seducing her. Still, it was a nice fantasy that she and her sister-in-law were cooking up. "He's just a man," she said nonchalantly. "I've resisted men who were better-looking than T. K. McKenna."

"Yeah," sighed Nina, "but they weren't T.K."

Patrice heard a muffled conversation, and then her brother was back on the line. "My wife was getting a little too worked up over that actor," he said jokingly. "And I did phone for a reason. Nina and I've got a few days off from work and school and thought we'd bring you the Jeep since we'll be coming over tomorrow."

"That'd be great," Patrice cried, touched by their thoughtfulness. She was going to have to fly back to Albuquerque and drive the car home if one of her brothers or sister hadn't offered. "You two haven't been out here in a while. You can make it a mini-vacation. I'll prepare the guest room. And I'll happily pay for your flight home."

"Don't worry about that," Patrick said. "We're doing okay. We can afford to pay for ourselves."

Patrice knew her brother was proud. Trying to give him a gift was like wrangling a steer. "You're going to be paying for the gasoline to get here. It's only fair that I pay for your flight back home."

"No, sis, save your money. You may not always have good years in Hollywood, you know. You don't want to wind up on a reality show."

Patrice laughed. Her brother worried about her career choice. She supposed she should thank her lucky stars that he was the only one in the family who thought she should have become a teacher, a doctor, a lawyer or anything else except an actor. It was the kind of talk she expected to get from her parents, but they were cool with her choice.

"Actually, Patrick, I could probably survive on what I made on my last film for the rest of my life if I left Hollywood and moved back to Albuquerque."

"Whoa," said Patrick, sounding genuinely impressed.

"No wonder everybody and his momma wants to be an actor."

"There are definite perks that come with success in this field," Patrice said. "So can your big sister pay for those plane tickets now?"

"Nah," said Patrick. She'd known it wasn't going to be that easy.

"Then I'll have to plan some really nice things to do while you're here," Patrice told him.

Nina, who must have been listening in, took the phone from Patrick. "You can introduce us to T.K.!"

"I hardly know the man," Patrice said, laughing.

Patrick took the phone back. "We're leaving early in the morning, sis. See you soon!"

"All right," Patrice said. "Love you both."

"Love you, too," Patrick said, his tone filled with laughter. Patrice imagined his wife was doing something to amuse him.

The last thing she heard before Patrick hung up was Nina's voice yelling, "Call him and invite him to dinner when we get there, Patty!"

Patrice laughed a while after hanging up. Phone T. K. McKenna and invite him over for steaks? Not hardly.

"Oh my gawd, Patty. You've redecorated since we were here last," exclaimed Nina upon seeing the living room. Patrice had replaced the old, worn living room furniture with custom made furnishings, and she had had French doors put in that led out to the big patio.

Otherwise the bungalow, built in the 1930s, and well-maintained over the years by its successive owners, was pretty much the same as it had been on their last visit.

Patrice was pleased by her sister-in-law's enthusiasm, though. She loved her home and was gratified when others liked it, too. Patrick picked her up in a bear hug while his wife made a circuit of the house. Patrick was six-three and a bit over two hundred pounds of muscle. He looked more like a cowboy than a college instructor, but when he opened his mouth to speak there was no denying he was a scholar.

"It's a trifle hot and muggy in L.A.," he said when he set her down.

"Oh, yeah," Patrice said jokingly. "The heat in Albuquerque is a *dry* heat, not this sticky stuff we have here." She had turned on the air, so it was nice and comfortable in the house.

Patrick, in a short-sleeved blue T-shirt and Wrangler jeans with his favorite pair of boots, followed her back to the kitchen when she began walking in that direction, talking the whole while. "How was the trip? Any problems?"

His boots made tapping noises on the kitchen's tile floor as he walked over to the table and sat down. At the stove, Patrice took the lid off a huge skillet filled with fresh chicken strips simmering in a spicy Southwestern sauce and gently stirred the mixture.

Patrick sniffed the air. "Smells good. What're you making, Mom's quesadillas?"

"I'm making chicken enchiladas. I like to let the chicken simmer in the sauce before rolling the filling in the corn tortillas and putting everything in the oven."

Nina came into the kitchen. She was a trim, petite twenty-two-year-old with beautiful dark brown skin and eyes the color of tea. Her black hair was natural, and she wore it in a short Afro. She was dressed similarly to her husband in jeans and a short-sleeved shirt, but she wore sandals instead of boots. She peered at the amount of food Patrice was preparing. "Looks like a lot for three people," she said, then wiggled her eyebrows at her sister-in-law in a suggestive manner. She sidled up to Patrice. "Don't you have his number?"

Patrice put the lid on the skillet and reached for the deep-dish glass baking dish she was going to put the enchiladas in. "Nina Sutton, you're like a mosquito that just won't quit buzzing around my head," she said with a laugh. "Yes, I have his number, but I'm not going to use it. I can't call him up and say, 'T.K., I'm making chicken enchiladas. Some of my family is visiting and just dying to meet you. Come on over!'"

"He'd probably be thrilled," Nina said. Her pretty face was animated. "How often do you think a woman like you invites him to a home-cooked meal? Probably never, and it's not as if you two would be alone. Patrick and I are here."

Patrick cleared his throat, and the two women turned to look at him. "Patty, it might not be a bad idea. I'd kind of like to get a look at the man you're going to be working with for the next few months."

"I can't believe my ears. You, too, Patrick?" Patrice cried.

"Well, Nina had some good points on the drive here. It's inevitable that you're going to be around an irresistible male, according to my wife. I'd like to feel him out. See what kind of vibes he gives off."

"This doesn't make me more willing to make that call, Patrick—not if you're going to be judging the guy all evening. Now I'm *really* afraid you and Nina are going to do something to embarrass me."

Patrick laughed. "Patty, I'm not the same boy who used to delight in chasing your dates off by being a pest. I'm a married man. I have a mortgage for goodness' sake."

Patrice gave Nina a stern look. "Do you think you can refrain from touching him, screaming your head off in his presence or doing anything else that might make him think my family's a bunch of lunatics?"

"Do you want the truth, or do you want me to tell you what you want to hear?" asked Nina.

"Then that answers my question," Patrice said, turning back to her cooking. "I'm not phoning him."

Nina sighed disappointedly. "Why can't I lie like everybody else?"

"If she gets out of control, I'll pick her up and carry her to the guest room," Patrick said firmly.

Nina looked at him and smiled. Her husband was

being a team player and backing her up. "You know Patrick's a man of his word."

"Oh, all right," Patrice relented. "Don't get your hopes up, though. He's a very busy man."

Chapter 5

"...I was only phoning to see how you were doing," T.K. said for the third time. For ten minutes, he'd been trying to say goodbye to Aisha without being rude.

"I thought I heard somebody trying to get in the back door last night," Aisha said. "This big old house is scary with just me in it. I never thought I'd say this, but I miss your parents."

"Did you see anybody?" T.K. asked, focusing on the problem, if indeed there was one.

"No, it was just my imagination," said Aisha with a sigh. "It must be my hormones, you know, the baby." She liked to remind him she was carrying Malcolm's child. It was her insurance, after all, for remaining a part of the family. T.K. thought that in a few months her insurance policy would be declared null and void once the paternity test was done.

However, he didn't want to upset a pregnant woman by saying that.

"You know how to set the alarm, and you're not really alone in the house. Mrs. Harrison is there." Alma Harrison was his parents' live-in housekeeper.

"She had the night off," Aisha griped. "She didn't get home until after midnight."

"I assure you that if anyone tried to break into the house, the police would be there before he got inside. You're safe, Aisha. Now, I have to go. Take care," T.K. said nicely.

She started to say something else, but T.K.'s cell phone began ringing—he'd phoned Aisha using the landline— and he quickly said, "That's my personal line, I've got to get that. Goodbye."

"Bye," said Aisha sultrily.

T.K. screwed up his face as though he smelled something bad. It made his skin crawl when she did that.

He quickly looked at the cell phone's display. Patrice Sutton. His afternoon was getting interesting. He pressed Talk and calmly spoke into the mouthpiece. "Patrice, this is a pleasant surprise. What can I do for you?"

On her end, Patrice's heart was beating rapidly. She was standing in the middle of her bedroom, having left Patrick and Nina in the kitchen so she would have a little privacy when she humiliated herself. She didn't believe T.K. was going to accept her invitation.

"Hi," she said softly. "I'm cooking, and…"

"You cook?" he asked, surprised.

"Yes, I'm making a Southwestern dish my mom used to make, and I realized that I'm making enough to feed a small army. I was wondering if, you know, you're not doing anything special tonight, if you'd like to come to dinner. I mean, I'd understand if you can't make it, but I thought I'd ask anyway."

"I'd love to," T.K. said immediately.

"My brother and his wife are my guests for a few days," Patrice warned. "They'll be here, too."

"Your brother from Albuquerque?" asked T.K., sounding intrigued.

"Yes, remember I told you I'd left my car in Albuquerque? He and Nina, that's his wife, drove it here so I wouldn't have to go get it."

"That was nice of them," T.K. said. "I'd love to meet them."

"Are you sure?" Patrice hedged, offering him an out. There was still time for him to gracefully turn down her invitation.

T.K. laughed. "I'm beginning to think you don't want me to come."

"No, that's not it," she denied. She lowered her voice, "It's just that there's no telling how they're going to react when they see you. They're big fans. I don't want you to feel like you're an attraction at the zoo."

"I'll bring the wine—red, white?" T.K. said with a chuckle.

"I'm making chicken enchiladas."

"White, it is," T.K. said. "Are you making the chicken enchiladas spicy?"

"Is there any other way?" Patrice joked.

"Not in my book. What time?"

"Seven," Patrice told him. "See you then."

"Yes, you will," T.K. said, and hung up.

Patrice was smiling when she closed her cell phone. She wondered why she was so happy. It wasn't as if this was a date.

She walked back into the kitchen with her head lowered and a dejected expression on her face. Nina came to her and rubbed her arm sympathetically. "He turned you down, huh?"

Patrice grinned as she raised her gaze to her sister-in-law's. "Gotcha! He'll be here at seven."

Nina's mouth fell open in amazement, and she was speechless, a condition that until now had never befallen her. Patrick laughed and went to pull her into his arms. "I don't like this," he said, peering into his wife's astonished face. He looked at Patrice. "Do you think she's okay?" He held Nina at arm's length and gently shook her. Nina was smiling, but she wasn't focusing.

Patrice laughed. "She'll snap out of it when she realizes that he'll be here in less than three hours."

Nina startled as if she'd been poked with a cattle prod. "Oh, I have to get ready. I need to shower and do my hair and makeup, and I didn't bring anything appropriate to wear. What was I thinking when I packed?" She turned her gaze on Patrice. "I'm gonna have to raid your closet."

"You're welcome to it," Patrice told her, still laughing softly. She calmly went back to preparing the meal.

Nina hurried from the kitchen presumably to start getting ready for T.K.'s arrival. Patrick followed mumbling, "I don't like this. I don't like it at all."

"Remember," Patrice said, "you wanted to meet him, too."

"Yeah, but look at her," Patrick complained. "She wasn't this excited on our wedding day!" He jogged to keep up with his wife.

When she was alone in the kitchen, Patrice took a deep breath and looked around the room. It was a beautiful space with beige Mexican tile, cherrywood cabinetry, granite countertops and stainless steel appliances. Although modern, it had a homey feel with touches of the Southwest in the form of clay pots and Native American art. Throughout her home, she had Native American and African inspired paintings, sculptures, clay pots and handmade blankets.

Her home was far from being a mansion, but it was lovingly cared for. She stopped herself. Why was she standing here obsessing about her home? She was not going to pull a Nina and lose her mind because T. K. McKenna was coming to dinner.

Besides, she had a meal to get on the table.

* * *

T.K. chose two bottles of good white wine from his wine cellar and put them in the refrigerator to chill shortly after he got off the phone with Patrice. On his way upstairs, he wondered if he should take Patrice some flowers. But, no, she had said this wasn't a date. It would look as if he thought it was a date if he did that.

Sam met him at the door of the cellar and peered up at him as if to ask what was up.

"I'm going out, boy," he told the dog. It sometimes embarrassed him that he talked to Sam like he was his friend instead of an animal. Sam seemed to enjoy it, so he continued to do so. "I've been invited to dinner. Can you believe it? I can't remember the last time anyone invited me to dinner without wanting something."

After he put the wine bottles in the refrigerator, he glanced up at the clock on the wall. If he left here in about two hours, he should have plenty of time to make it to Patrice's by seven. There was time for a shower and a shave. He hadn't asked her if the dress was casual, but he assumed that it was. She wouldn't dress up for dinner with her family unless it was a special occasion, would she?

Two hours later, he left the house by the downstairs garage door. He was wearing jeans and a nice shirt with his favorite pair of Nike shoes. In the garage, he stood for a moment considering which car to drive. He definitely didn't want to pull up to Patrice's house in an Italian sports car. Nor did he feel the SUV was appropriate. He didn't want her brother to think he was flaunting the fact that he could afford a sixty-thousand-dollar sports utility vehicle. That left the black muscle car. It was a restored 1968 Chevrolet Camaro SS. He'd done the work himself, with the aid of a professional restorer. The good thing about his vocation was that whenever he wanted to learn to do something, he could afford the best instructors.

He looked at his work as an opportunity to learn. For example, he'd been taking martial arts lessons for the past decade because he'd needed to know a little about martial arts for a role in a film.

He'd never been to college. He considered life to be his university, and he devoted himself to a discipline whenever he had an interest in it. That's why he was a third-degree black belt in karate.

The Camaro purred to life, and he backed it out of the garage. Sunday evening in Malibu was ideal. The air was warm, and a breeze coming off the ocean brought the smell of night jasmine wafting in. At dusk, the sun was an orange ball disappearing into the Pacific.

He turned onto the highway and accelerated. The car handled like a dream. It was his favorite. He smiled. It had been Malcolm's favorite, too. His smile vanished. Memories of his brother were happy and sad simultaneously. He should have had a long life. Instead, it had been cut short at thirty-three. He should have known true love. Instead, he had fallen in love with a woman whose intentions had been less than honorable. It angered him that Malcolm hadn't had a better time while he'd been here.

He checked himself. How did he know Malcolm wasn't happy? There wasn't a day that he didn't hear his brother's laughter. Maybe he was happy. Maybe Aisha had been the love of his life. He supposed that after Malcolm died he'd had to take his frustrations out on somebody and he'd targeted Aisha. For all he knew, Aisha could be innocent. She could be telling the truth when she said Malcolm was the father of her child. Time would tell.

As he drove, he forced himself to think of the evening ahead. He didn't want his melancholy thoughts to intrude on the evening. He was going to see Patrice again, a woman who was lovely, innocent and still untouched by Hollywood. He could see it in her eyes—the joy she derived from her craft. When she acted, she embodied the character she portrayed. Technically, she was close to flawless. He didn't think anyone was perfect, but those whom he believed got pretty close were Denzel and Robert DeNiro. Patrice was actually just getting started in the business. However, she had something a lot of young actresses didn't possess: talent.

He tried to tell himself that was the only reason he'd been excited when she'd phoned—she was an up-and-coming talent, and it was always fascinating to watch someone like her grow as an actor. However, he was not the type of man to delude himself. He had gotten excited as soon as he'd heard her voice because he was attracted to her. Take away the talent, and she was still a very intriguing woman. Yes, he was physically attracted to her. She, frankly, made him sweat. There was something else below the surface that drew him to her. He couldn't put his finger on it yet. Finding out what it was would take some investigating. He instinctively knew that getting to know her better would be a pleasurable experience.

Patrice was pulling her dress over her head when someone knocked on her bedroom door. She smoothed the dress over her hips and called, "Come in!"

Nina strode into the room. She was still in her bathrobe. She gasped when she saw Patrice. "You're wearing that?"

Patrice glanced down at her dress. It was pale yellow and made from a cotton material that was soft and smooth and felt wonderful against her skin. Sleeveless, it was scoop-necked and displayed a modest amount of cleavage. Her arms, which were two of her best features, looked lovely in this dress. The hem fell a couple inches above her knees, showing off her toned legs, and it was cinched at the waist. "I like this dress," she told Nina, peering at her with a disapproving expression.

"I like it, too," Nina said, frowning. "But it looks like you're going to a picnic or something, not dinner with a guy."

"That's good," Patrice said, moving around Nina to go to her vanity where she sat down, put a towel around her shoulders and began applying a bit of blush and lipstick.

She'd moisturized after her shower and didn't think she needed to wear any makeup other than the blush and the lipstick, so she'd forego the foundation.

Nina stood next to her with a look of consternation on her pretty face. "Can't you put on something more... seductive?"

Patrice met her sister-in-law's eyes in the mirror. She burst out laughing. "Do you think I would try to seduce T.K. in front of you and Patrick?"

Nina turned away. "What if Patrick and I retired early? It was a long drive from Albuquerque."

Then Patrice knew what her sister-in-law had been planning all along. She and Patrick were going to disappear once the evening got underway so that she and T.K. could be alone.

Patrice rose and went to stand directly in front of Nina. "Listen to me, Nina Sutton. If you and Patrick claim you're exhausted and try to go to bed before dessert I'm going to feign tiredness, too, and T.K. will have no alternative but to go home. Do you hear me? I can't believe you were thinking of doing that!"

Pouting, Nina stomped from the room. "I try to do something nice for my sister-in-law, and look where it gets me—yelled at!"

"I'm not yelling," Patrice pointed out.

"You'd just as well be," Nina said. She turned around at the door and thought she'd give it a last-ditch effort.

"What are you afraid of? That you'll like him, and then you'll have to revise your never-get-involved-with-someone-I-work-with rule?"

Patrice sighed. She knew Nina meant well. She loved her for wanting to see her find someone to share her life with. But T. K. McKenna was not ripe for the picking, no matter what Nina thought.

"Sweetie," she said gently as she went to place a hand on Nina's shoulder. "I know you love me and you want to see me as happy as you and Patrick are, but T.K. has been through some emotional upheavals recently. If I'm not mistaken, he found out Edina Edwards was cheating on him about the same time his brother was killed in an accident."

"Oh, my God, I forgot about that," Nina cried. Patrice smiled. Nina sounded as though her card in the T. K. McKenna Fan Club was going to be revoked because she'd forgotten an important event in his life.

"Yes, well," Patrice continued, "he's vulnerable right now. I think he'd appreciate a friend more than a lover."

Nina was all seriousness. "You're right." She smiled at Patrice. "Forget everything I said." She took a deep breath. "I'd better go get dressed. It's almost seven."

Just as Nina finished her sentence, the doorbell rang. T.K. was early. Nina squealed and shot out the door, making a beeline for the guest room. Patrick, who had long ago showered and dressed, met her in the hallway. Patrice stepped into the hallway. "Patrick, would you mind getting the door? I'm not quite finished getting ready." She still had to put on her sandals and comb her hair.

"No problem," Patrick said and headed for the front door.

After he had rung the bell, T.K. stood on the tiny porch with a wine bottle in each hand. The door swung open, and he knew disappointment must have briefly registered on his face because he had expected Patrice to answer it. Instead, a young man about his size held the door open and took a step back so he could enter. "Hey, man," he said in a deep voice. T.K. handed him one of the wine bottles so he'd have one free hand with which to shake his hand. They shook hands and grinned at each other.

"You must be Patrice's brother," T.K. said as he stepped inside.

"Patrick," Patrick said. "Good to meet you, Mr. McKenna."

T.K. peered at him. He was young, maybe twenty-five or less. He probably referred to all of his elders in the manner in which he'd addressed him. God, he felt old.

He laughed shortly. "T.K.'ll do," he told him.

Patrick closed the door and faced him. "Patrice and Nina are still getting dressed."

T.K. handed him the other bottle of wine. "I'm a little early."

He was five minutes early. The drive had been so pleasant that he'd lost track of time. After he had dispelled sad thoughts, his mind had been busy wondering if his memory of Patrice was accurate. How would he feel when he saw her again? That's why he'd been somewhat disappointed when Patrick had answered the door.

"You're not early," Patrick said. "You're on time. But you know women have to keep you waiting, no matter what time you arrive." He led him back to the kitchen where he put the wine in the refrigerator.

T.K. admired the way Patrice had decorated the place. It was plain to see she loved her home and took pride in it. It was a very welcoming space, warm and inviting, kind of like her—assuming, of course, his first impression of her had been correct.

The aromas in the air were mouthwatering, and the table had been set for four. Patrick said, "Would you like something to drink? I think there's beer in fridge."

"If you're having one, I'll take one," T.K. said.

Patrick got a Corona for each of them from the refrigerator and popped the lids off the bottles with an opener that was stuck on the fridge door by a magnet.

He handed a bottle to T.K. "They shouldn't be too much longer."

Patrick felt ill-equipped to entertain a movie star. He wished his sister had been dressed so that she could have answered the door. What was he supposed to do while they waited for the women to put in an appearance?

They stood awkwardly next to the refrigerator for a couple minutes. Then Patrick said, "There must be something on ESPN. Wanna check it out while we wait?"

T.K. said that he would, and they went to the living room where Patrick turned on the TV and they sat on the sofa and watched soccer. That's where Patrice and Nina found them a few minutes later when they joined them.

"Good evening, T.K.," Patrice said, smiling warmly. Behind her, Nina stifled a squeal of delight.

T.K. rose. "Hello, Patrice." Their eyes met, and he was instantly reminded of the expectant, wholly unsettling feeling he'd had the last time he was alone with her. Her beautiful wide-spaced brown eyes were lit with humor, and as his eyes lowered to her mouth, she moistened her lips and he sighed involuntarily. Thank God Patrick had the TV volume up. No one could have heard him.

She placed her sister-in-law in front of her. "This is Nina, Patrick's wife."

T.K. offered Nina his hand. "It's good to meet you, Nina."

"Hello," Nina said shyly with downcast eyes. Her voice was barely audible.

T.K. bent down. She was a tiny girl. Her husband must have been an entire foot taller than she was. "So, how long have you and Patrick been married? You both look so young. You can't have been married long."

Nina smiled, revealing dimples in both cheeks. She finally met his eyes. "Nine months," she said softly, eyes sparkling with happiness.

"Newlyweds," said T.K. enthusiastically. "Congratulations on your marriage."

"Thank you," Nina said. Patrick got up and stood behind Nina and wrapped his arms around her. "She's a keeper," he said fondly.

Nina beamed her pleasure.

Patrice was happy that Nina had been able to avoid embarrassment when she met T.K. *She* had felt like squealing with excitement upon seeing him herself. Years of training at Juilliard had come in handy.

Her whole body was tingling. She wanted to grab him, kiss him and run her hands all over his bald head. What was wrong with her? Each time she saw him, her body went crazy, and she had to rein in her girlish tendencies toward throwing herself in his arms and pressing her body against his. Was it pheromones? Whatever it was he had, it was so strong she was barely able to resist. How was she going to get through dinner, let alone months of filming in Wyoming?

She could admit it: her attraction to him was growing. Her initial attraction, the day of the interview in Mark Greenberg's office, had been strong, but this was bordering on overpowering.

"Well," she said breathlessly, after a brief silence during which they all stood around and smiled at one another, "dinner's ready!"

Chapter 6

"Careful," Patrice cautioned T.K. as he was about to put a forkful of the main dish in his mouth. "I made it with several kinds of hot peppers. It could be an acquired taste for you."

T.K. thought it was sweet of her to be concerned, but he considered himself somewhat of an *aficionado* of foods of a spicy nature. He munched on raw jalapeno peppers just to add flavor to the experience whenever he ate steamed crabs, one of his favorite foods. Wasabi didn't faze him. He put the food in his mouth and withdrew the fork. He let it remain on his tongue a second so that he could discern the various flavors. It was delicious, peppery and definitely a tomato-based sauce, with a hint of sweetness. That was the top note. He chewed. The chicken was tender, the corn tortilla wrapping a delight.

As for hotness, it was moderate at best. He smiled at Patrice. "It's the best chicken enchilada I've ever had."

Patrice blushed. "It's my mom's recipe."

He continued to eat. Across the table, Nina and Patrick were watching him as though they expected him to expectorate any second now and dash to the sink to stick his mouth beneath the faucet and gulp mouthfuls of cold water.

He laughed. "I'm all right, really," he assured them.

They laughed too and tucked into their meals. "It's just that we're used to hot peppers," Nina said. "My momma puts them in everything—breakfast, lunch and dinner. She even makes pepper jelly to eat with her collard greens when she cooks them."

"I had that once when I was in New Orleans," T.K. said. "It's sweet but very spicy. Good stuff." He made short work of the chicken enchiladas on his plate and didn't once reach for his glass of wine or the glass of water in front of him.

"Would you like more?" Patrice asked, rising.

"Yes, please," he said, holding his plate while she placed another serving onto it from the baking dish on the table.

"What do you two do?" he asked Patrick and Nina, as he started in on his second helping.

"I teach English at the University of New Mexico," said Patrick after swallowing.

"And I'm a law student," said Nina.

"You teach at the university level?" T.K. asked, surprised. "Excuse me, but how old *are* you?"

"I'll be twenty-five next month," said Patrick. T.K. thought he sounded like someone who'd been asked that question a lot. He hadn't meant to offend him.

"He's the youngest instructor at the university with a doctorate degree," said Patrice proudly, smiling at her brother.

"I envy you," said T.K. sincerely.

Patrick's brows rose in surprise. "You envy *me?*"

"You're only twenty-five, and you know exactly what you want to do with your life," T.K. explained. "I'm thirty-six, and I still don't know."

Patrick laughed. "You seem to be doing pretty well to me."

"I'm in the business of make-believe," T.K. said with a smile. "If I do my job right, for two hours, I'm able to make the audience believe I'm whomever I'm portraying at that given moment. Then I'm on to the next project. If I'm good at what I do, I'm paid well and that's a bonus, but I wouldn't refer to this as a calling. You, on the other hand, probably feel as though teaching English is what you were born to do."

Patrick was nodding with a contemplative expression on his face. "I love it," he said.

Nina gasped. "You don't love acting?" she asked.

"Love it?" asked T.K., frowning. "It's something I'm good at, and right now I'm in demand. It's a business. I wouldn't say I'm passionate about it."

Patrice was astonished by this revelation. With every T. K. McKenna film she'd seen, she had been convinced that the actor on the screen was totally into his craft— that he lived and breathed acting. He was a chameleon. How could someone fake that?

"Did you lose the passion, or you've never really felt it?" asked Patrice.

T.K. put down his fork. He didn't want to disillusion Patrice because it was quite obvious to him that she did feel passionate about acting. They were different in that regard, however, and he thought he should be honest with her.

Looking into her eyes, he said, "You have to under-stand that where I grew up it was all about the hustle. Yes, my parents were teachers. They tried their best to keep me out of trouble, but the guys I associated with were not the sort they thought I should be hanging with. My parents wanted me to go to college. I had the grades. But the people I identified with were the kind who found a hustle, worked it and brought in big bucks by doing that, and often what they were doing wasn't exactly legal. I got into acting by accident. They were shooting a DeNiro film in the neighborhood, and they were looking for extras. I happened to meet DeNiro, and he liked the look of me. He had the writers give me a couple lines. After that, I was hooked. Here was a hustle I thought I could work. So, at eighteen I took off for L.A."

"That's not what I read about you," Patrice said, puzzled. "According to your background, you went to a performing arts high school in New York. You always knew you wanted to be an actor."

"Manufactured by my first agent," T.K. told her. "She thought it sounded better."

"She was right!" Nina said, and they all laughed.

T.K. continued to meet Patrice's gaze. "Are you disappointed?"

She smiled at him. "I'm even more impressed with you than I was before."

This warmed T.K.'s heart. His eyes were watering. He blinked. His *eyes* were watering! And his tongue was on fire. He reached for his glass of water and drank deeply.

Patrice smiled innocently. "Those peppers have a cumulative effect, I'm afraid. They sneak up on you."

Nina and Patrick laughed. Patrice rose and went to the refrigerator to get some ice for T.K.'s glass of water. It seemed to help when those particular peppers kicked in.

She put some ice into his glass, and T.K. gratefully drank some of it, allowing pieces of ice to remain on his tongue. He felt some relief, but his tongue was still burning.

"I think I'll serve dessert," Patrice said helpfully. Dessert was vanilla bean ice cream with caramel sauce. The milk in the ice cream effectively put out the fire in the peppers. Ice cream was a common dessert in their household when hot peppers were served with dinner.

"What's wrong with you people?" T.K. asked, looking

at each of them in turn. "Have hot peppers burned off your taste buds? Why aren't you burning?"

Nina smiled sweetly. "Like I said, we eat peppers for breakfast, lunch and dinner. Actually, they're good for you, excellent for keeping your sinuses clear."

"I'm amazed you still have sinuses," T.K. exclaimed.

Momentarily, Patrice served each of them a bowl of ice cream. She sat beside T.K., spooned some of his and held it out for him to eat. "I'm so sorry. I'm a terrible hostess. I should have known you weren't ready for Albuquerque hotness."

T.K.'s eyes met hers. He accepted the spoonful of ice cream from her and took the spoon. Burning tongue or not, he wanted to kiss her until her eyes rolled back in her head. "Thank you," he said after swallowing the delicious dessert. The effect of the ice cream on his tongue was instantaneous. The burning subsided. He smiled.

She smiled back at him, her lovely eyes lowering seductively. His heart thudded. His groin tightened, and he was glad he was sitting down. "Forgive me?" she asked softly.

"Just about anything," he returned, equally softly.

Across from them, Nina was grinning. She grasped her husband's hand. "I knew there was something there," she whispered.

But a brother is never happy to see a man look at his sister the way T. K. McKenna was looking at her. He knew exactly what was on the actor's mind, and it wasn't anything as noble as marriage.

After conversation over coffee, T.K. insisted on helping Patrice with the dishes. Nina played the "I'm exhausted" card in spite of the earlier threat from Patrice. As she and Patrick were leaving the kitchen, Patrice thought he looked reluctant to leave. She was miffed with Nina, but what could she do about it now? She vowed to get revenge later.

Like most cooks in her family, Patrice cleaned as she cooked, so there were no pots and pans to wash following the meal—only the plates, dishes and silverware they had used. These she put into a sink of hot soapy water and began washing while T.K. rinsed them and set them on the draining board to air dry.

"Those chicken enchiladas were delicious even if they did make my eyes water," he said as they worked companionably side by side.

"Well, now if the director wants you to cry on cue, you know exactly what to eat to get those results," she joked.

T.K. wondered if this was a snide remark about his apparent regard for acting not as an art form but simply a job that paid the bills. For some reason the thought of her holding him in contempt because he wasn't as passionate about acting as she was pained him.

"Was that said to elicit a laugh, or do you really think

less of me because I don't believe acting is the be all and end all of my existence?"

Patrice washed and handed him the last plate. "I don't think acting is everything either," she told him, looking him straight in the eyes. "What? You think I think less of you because I went to Juilliard and you didn't?"

T.K. rinsed the plate and stacked it on the rack atop the draining board with the other dishes. Then he dried his hands on the dish towel and handed the towel to her. He gave her his full attention. "No, I don't." He frowned. "I don't know, maybe I do. Women are always making assumptions about me based on what they see in movie theaters. I'm an honest kind of guy. I don't like pretense. I've met so many people who told me one thing and meant another. I don't have time for that anymore, Patrice. I don't care if you hurt my feelings. Be honest with me. Are you disappointed because I'm not what you thought I was?"

Patrice grasped him by the arm and moved close to him. "T.K., I don't know you well enough to have formed an opinion of you. What you told me about your lack of passion for acting was surprising, but it didn't make me any less attracted to you as a person. I was raised to be tolerant of differences in people. That applies to race, sexual orientation and, yes, the amount of passion someone has for his work." She laughed suddenly. If he only knew how she really felt about him at this moment, he wouldn't worry at all about her regard for him.

He smiled down at her. "What was that laugh for?"

His back was to the sink. Patrice pressed the length of her body against his. His arms went around her waist and he held her, just held her. Patrice placed her ear against his chest and listened to his heartbeat. It was strong and steady. It's how she felt about him at this instance. "I like you so much. I wish I weren't about to do a film with you," she told him.

"Why is that?" he asked quietly.

"Because I'm hopelessly drawn to you. I actually ache to be close to you. But I don't get involved with men I work with." She raised her eyes to his. "Is that honest enough for you?"

T.K. bent and gently touched his mouth to hers. Her sweet breath mingled with his, and she pressed back. This he took as an invitation and gave her the full assault.

She tasted wonderful, like warmth personified. He felt that kiss all the way down to his feet and back up again. It made his body feel more alive than it had felt in months, and for that reason alone, he could have stood there kissing her for quite some time. But the effect was also arousing, and he could not press his body against hers for much longer without her detecting that he wanted more from her than a mere kiss. When they parted, Patrice slowly opened her eyes and sighed. T.K. smiled at her.

"Technically, we're not working together yet," he said. "But I'm a patient man, and I'm willing to honor your wishes. When you say you don't get involved, what do you mean? Explain yourself, and be specific."

He was looking at her so intensely that Patrice knew he was serious and not simply humoring her on this subject. "I can't kiss you?" he asked. His eyes lowered to her mouth. "Because I would die if I couldn't kiss you again."

What was Patrice supposed to say to that? The fact was she had avoided getting involved with her leading men in any way, shape or form. When she had worked on the sitcom, the lead actor was married, but that didn't stop his having affairs with his costars. It was rumored that it was his goal to sleep with every female in the cast. She and another actress were the only two out of six women who hadn't been seduced by him. When some casts of sitcoms claimed to be like one big happy family when they accepted awards on award shows, they weren't kidding. As for the two leading men she'd played opposite in her two theatrical releases, one was faithful to his wife and the other was not. She had to avoid being alone with him because he had a habit of grabbing her and saying, "You want me. You're just playing hard to get." Impossible to get was closer to the truth. She had been relieved when that film had wrapped.

She decided to tell T.K. the truth. "In the past, I've never even kissed a costar. In some ways, I look at working the way you do. I just want to do my job and go home. I have not wanted an on-set romance that can get messy when one of you doesn't feel as strongly about the other. I've witnessed a few of those."

"Comes with the territory," T.K. agreed. He winced

when Edina's image came to mind. "I started my last relationship on location. That didn't end well." He met her eyes again. "That doesn't mean I believe the same thing would happen to us, if you decided to relax your rules in my favor."

"Are you asking me to?" Patrice ventured.

"Are you asking me to ask you to?" he cautiously countered.

Patrice narrowed her eyes at him. Was he playing it safe now after all that talk about honesty? He needed to tell her what he wanted from her, and he needed to be specific just like he'd asked her to be. "Spell it out," she told him. "Three weeks from now we're going to be in Wyoming. By the way, why so soon? Mark didn't mention that. Usually I have several months to report to work after the contract's been negotiated. Luckily I was available."

"The actress who was to portray Bella got pregnant, and she backed out at the last minute," T.K. said.

"Who is she?"

"Dina Thompson."

"I like her," said Patrice. "She would have done a good job. So I'm second choice."

"Does that rankle?" he asked, thigh to thigh with her.

She laughed shortly. "No, I'm lucky everything turned out the way it did."

"That's how I feel about it," T.K. said, bending to kiss her again.

This time Patrice rose onto tiptoes, wrapped her arms around his neck and finally fulfilled a secret wish; she wound up with her hands caressing his bald head and the delicious sensation she was rewarded with was even better than she'd imagined.

T.K. smiled when she released him. "Can you tell me you can resist doing that for the entire time we're on location?"

Patrice took a deep breath and stepped backward, regarding him with clear eyes. "I admit rubbing your head is nearly orgasmic it feels so good, but yes, I can, and I will avoid doing it when we're on location."

"Well, you're a stronger person than I am," T.K. complimented her. He couldn't believe he was about to do this, but he wasn't going to simply lie down and take defeat either. He wanted her in his arms. He wanted her in his life, and eventually he wanted her in his bed. If he left it up to her and her exalted sense of a work ethic, they might never get together.

"I'll tell you what," he suggested sweetly. "If while we're on location you can resist kissing me, when not doing so in the course of your job, then fine, we'll stick to your rules. However, should you kiss me, of your own free will at any time, then it's on. We, as you put it, will 'get involved' while on location."

Patrice considered him for a while. That rugged square-jawed face, that smooth golden-brown skin, to say nothing of those lips, those eyes and her favorite feature—his bald head. His hard body was oh so enticing, but what lay between his ears was even more compelling. He was intellectually stimulating as well, and a thinking man always turned her on. He thought he could outmaneuver her. Was that overconfidence on his part? Or conceit? Had he been one of the top actors in the world for so long that he thought he was irresistible to every woman on the planet? She might need to take him down a peg or two.

She offered him her hand to shake. "You've got a deal."

T.K. accepted her hand but used it to pull her into his embrace, whereupon he kissed her until she nearly swooned in his arms. Patrice peered up at him after he let her go. "You play dirty."

"It's the only way," T.K. told her with a mischievous smile. "I'd better be going before Patrick comes back out to see what I'm doing to his sister. I saw that look he gave me as he and Nina were leaving the room."

Patrice walked him outside. "One more thing," she told him after she'd pulled the door closed behind them. "I can't see you again until we're on location."

"What?" T.K. exclaimed, none too happy with her announcement. "We've got three weeks before we go to Wyoming!"

She smiled. "Don't you see? Absence makes the heart grow fonder. This is to your advantage. Surely after experiencing your kisses and then being deprived of them for three weeks I'll be ready to fall into your arms once we get to Wyoming."

"You're an evil woman, Patrice Sutton."

"Wait a minute," Patrice said, thinking. "If I lose the bet, you get, well, me. But if I'm able to resist you, what do I get?"

"I hadn't thought about that because I'm not going to lose," T.K. told her honestly. "However, you have a point. Name it, and it's yours."

Patrice spied the car parked at the curb. She walked over to it and ran her hand across its hood. It was a beauty. "Is this a Camaro?"

"Yes, it is," T.K. said with a note of pride. "It's a 1968 Chevrolet Camaro SS. I restored her myself."

"Then she means a lot to you?" Patrice asked speculatively.

"She's my favorite," he confirmed.

"I'll take *her* if you lose the bet," Patrice told him.

Even though his heart skipped a beat in shock and disappointment at her demand, T.K. didn't protest. "I'm not going to lose the bet because you're going to want to kiss me every minute of every day while we're on location."

"Don't hold your breath!" Patrice said with a laugh as she turned to go back inside. "Good night, Trevor Kennedy McKenna."

"Good night, Ms. Sutton," he said grimly. Let her think she'd won that round.

T.K. chuckled after he got behind the wheel of the Camaro and started the engine. He liked her spirit. He had no intention of losing the bet!

Chapter 7

Three weeks later, Patrice arrived in Casper, Wyoming. She drove through one of the city's main thoroughfares, looking for the name of the street of the inn where the cast and crew would be staying. She'd flown in to the Casper/Natrona County International Airport and rented a car. She would have driven the nearly nine hundred miles, but then she'd realized that if she had she would be driving back home in the snow in December when filming was supposed to end. She didn't like driving in the snow.

Soon, she found the inn and pulled the Ford Focus into the parking lot. It was eighty degrees out, and the sun felt wonderful on her skin as she walked to the inn's entrance.

"Hey, Patrice, you made it!" a male voice called from

across the parking lot. Patrice removed her sunglasses and smiled at Mark Greenberg. "Mark, yes, a day ahead of schedule. Has anyone else arrived yet besides you and I?"

Mark, looking relaxed in a golf shirt, khaki slacks and athletic shoes, came and gave her a quick hug. "A few," he said. "But I don't expect most of them until tomorrow just in time for the first meeting."

Patrice knew what he said was true. She liked to arrive a day early so that she would be well-rested and sharp during the meeting about the shooting schedule. Smiling up at him, she asked, "Any sign of T.K.?"

Even though she and T.K. had not seen each other in three weeks, they had stayed in touch by phone, and he had told her he would be arriving today. He was driving because he wanted to bring Sam with him, and Sam hated air travel.

He left the dog with a friend or his parents when he had to be out of the country, but when at all possible, he took Sam with him on location.

"Not yet," Mark told her. "It's early. He'll probably get here before dark." He gestured toward the inn's entrance with a nod of his head. "Come on. Let's get you checked in. Then, if you're not too tired, we can go get some lunch."

"I *am* a little travel-weary," Patrice told him. She turned, and he placed a protective hand at the small of her back. "So, you and T.K. have gotten to know each other?"

Patrice smiled. "Yes, a little," she said, leaving it at that. They'd spoken every day since he'd come to dinner that night, and she thought she knew him quite well by now—so much so that she could barely contain her eagerness to see him again. No, she was not going to make it easy for him to win their bet by leaping into his arms and kissing him hello. But she wasn't going to be too hard on herself if she couldn't resist giving him a hug or three.

Mark opened the door for her and admired the shape of her bottom in her jeans. With her jeans, she was wearing a sleeveless white cotton blouse that buttoned up front. Mark looked down at her feet—cowboy boots. She would definitely fit in around here. He'd never seen so many people wearing them before, and he'd been to Texas twice.

At the desk in the beautifully decorated lobby that had a highly polished hardwood floor and an Italian marble front desk, the clerk took her name, checked her registration and handed her a key card. "Your room is all ready for you, Ms. Sutton," said the young man, smiling warmly.

A few minutes later, Patrice was opening the blinds in the suite to allow some light inside while her bags were being placed at the foot of the bed by a strapping young man with blond hair. She tipped him when he was done and locked the door behind him.

With a sigh, she threw herself onto the bed and lay flat on her back looking at the ceiling for a few minutes.

She had declined Mark's lunch invitation in favor of a nap. She'd been up since four o'clock this morning, and tiredness was finally coming down on her. He'd looked disappointed when she had told him she preferred sleep to food right now. She hoped it had only been a friendly invitation between colleagues. Mark seemed sweet, but it was T.K. who fascinated her. He'd talked to her about his brother Malcolm and how devastated he and his family had been when he'd died. She had been so touched that she'd wanted to hop in her car and drive to Malibu to comfort him. They had talked for hours that night. She told him that although she had lost her grandparents to death, she couldn't imagine what he was going through because their transition had not been unexpected. Her grandparents had prepared the family for their deaths by living long lives and planning their own funerals. In the case of her grandmother, Ina, every detail had been planned down to what kind of flowers would drape her casket to the desire not to have a funeral but a wake at which the family would celebrate her life and not mourn her passing. Malcolm's death, however, had been unexpected and a shock to his family.

They had also discussed their last relationships. He told her he'd had suspicions that Edina was not with him out of love long before he'd discovered her many infidelities.

"It's one of the things you have to be wary of in this town," he'd said. "People are willing to do anything to get and stay in the limelight. Unfortunately, celebrity is not based on talent anymore. You can be a celebrity simply by association or by being notorious."

Patrice had to agree. Today, women and men, who'd had affairs with prominent people, could wind up with their own reality shows and bring in millions of dollars of revenue. Or by virtue of giving birth to multiple babies, you could have people all over the world observing your life 24/7.

She told him about Andre, whom she had loved and thought was the man she would spend the rest of her life with. He was not in the business. She'd met him at a restaurant he co-owned in Los Angeles. Initially, he told her he had never been married. Months later, after she was already in love with him, she had learned that not only had he been married before but the co-owner of the restaurant was his ex-wife. They had not been able to agree on who would get the restaurant in the divorce settlement. Both had been so vehement about hanging on to it that they were still hanging on to it. Because they still worked closely together practically every day, their love had been rekindled, which left Patrice out in the cold. She could not hate Andre, though. Even though he'd broken her heart and lied to her about never having been married, at least he'd done it by getting back together with his first love. They were remarried now.

"Are you sure you don't have any hard feelings for him?" T.K. had asked. "He lied, and then he started fooling around with his ex-wife while he was with you."

"When I found out he'd lied about his ex-wife, yes, I wanted to dropkick him into the middle of next week, but after I thought about it I wondered why I was upset. He loved her. My moaning and groaning wasn't going to change that fact. Sometimes you have to simply let go."

T.K. had sighed but had grudgingly agreed with her. "I just wish I'd given up on Edina long before the world found out about her extracurricular activities."

"It'll take time, but you'll forget the hurt one day and thank God you didn't marry her," Patrice had returned.

He'd laughed. "Yeah, thank God for that!"

Patrice fell asleep while reminiscing about that particular conversation. When she awakened it was late afternoon, the sun had gone behind a cloud and the room was in shadows. She sat up and switched on the bedside lamp. Golden light illuminated the dark corners of the room. Rising, she went to the bathroom, used it and stood in front of the mirror to assess the damage. Her short black hair was sticking up on her head at weird angles, and she had the imprint of the bedspread on her left cheek where she'd lain on it. Wide, dark eyes laughed at her reflection. "You're why actresses have professional makeup artists on the payroll," she said.

Her cell phone rang, and she hurried out to the bedroom and snatched it from the side pocket of her purse. She squinted at the display. It was T.K.

"Are you here yet?" she asked anxiously.

He laughed. "Sam and I are downstairs checking

in. What are you up to? I'm starved and want to get something to eat before crashing."

"What's your room number? I need to shower and dress, but I can meet you in twenty."

"Sounds good, it's number 101," said T.K. "Then you can give me a hello kiss."

"I'd rather kiss Sam."

"He'd appreciate that. He hasn't had a good kiss in ages," T.K. quipped.

Patrice laughed. "See you soon."

In the lobby, T.K. closed his cell phone and peered down at Sam. "She wants me."

T.K. answered the door with a towel wrapped around his waist. Patrice took a sharp intake of breath and tried to pretend she hadn't been affected by the sight of him standing there nearly naked. They didn't refer to him as "the body" for nothing. Arm, chest, stomach and leg muscles were beautifully defined. Still a bit damp from his shower, he looked like one of those oiled-up bodybuilders she saw on the beach. "There was no bathrobe in the room, and I can't find the one I brought with me," were T.K.'s first words as she walked into the room and he shut the door. "I'll only be a minute," he continued as he turned and went into the walk-in closet of the big suite, leg and thigh muscles flexing enticingly.

A beautiful golden retriever approached her, his tail wagging. "Oh, that's Sam," T.K. called to her.

Patrice knelt and hugged Sam. He made happy noises

as she rubbed his head and scratched him under the chin. "Aren't you a handsome boy," she cooed.

T.K. found them on the floor when he came into the room in jeans and a T-shirt. "Can I get some love?" he asked as he reached for her hand and pulled her up.

They hugged tightly. Patrice enjoyed the feel of his hard body cradling hers. She looked into his eyes. *God, I missed you,* she wanted to tell him, but that would only strengthen his belief that he was going to win the bet. "You look well," she said, a smile playing at the corners of her mouth.

"I missed you like crazy," T.K. told her plainly, not caring one whit about the bet.

"I missed you too!" she cried, and hugged him again.

He bent and nuzzled her neck. "For nine hundred miles, I thought of nothing but seeing you again."

She melted. She ached to kiss him. Hugging was nice, but there was nothing comparable to a heartfelt kiss—to taste him, breathe him in, feel his tongue enter her mouth and claim hers. She wanted to give herself to him.

When she felt his mouth on the side of her neck, she came to her senses. In the space of five minutes, he had her about to cave in to his desires. Oh, he was good, really good!

She disentangled herself from him and took a couple steps back. "That's enough, I'm only human. Let's go if we're going." She picked up her purse from the bed where she'd tossed it upon entering the room.

T.K. looked at her with hooded eyes. It was impossible for her to read his emotions at that point, but she was pretty sure he wasn't pleased. After a moment, he smiled. "This isn't going to be easy, is it?"

Patrice shook her head, no. "Now, put on your shoes, and let's go."

She played with Sam while he sat on the bed. "My plan backfired," he admitted after he'd gotten one sock on. "In three weeks, I'm ready to surrender and wave the white flag. There is *no* way I can work with you from late August until late December without kissing you. I'm weak."

Patrice didn't move. Sam had turned over onto his back, and she was rubbing his belly. A look of ecstasy was on the dog's mug.

T.K. envied him.

She waited until he had both shoes on, and then she rose and gave Sam a parting pat on the head. "Good boy," she said to Sam. She walked over to T.K. and pulled him off the bed. "From now on, I want you to be a good boy." Her hand was on his chest. "I'd like to rip your clothes off right now and make love to you until we're both too weak to move. But that kind of behavior would compromise my principles, and I do have principles. My parents raised me right. I don't jump into bed with someone I've known for a month. If you want me, you're going to have to prove to me that when I give myself to you, I'll be doing the right thing with the right man. You know my history."

T.K. liked the fact that she had principles. He was not

without them himself. "What has that got to do with a kiss?" he asked.

"Because a kiss is the prelude to intimacy, and in and of itself, it *is* intimate." She gave him a knowing look. "How long do you think it would be before we'd be in bed if we started kissing each other at every opportunity, thrown together, as we are, up here in lonely Wyoming? You know I'm right."

"You have a point," T.K. conceded. "But, damn, woman, take cold showers or something." He put his wallet in his pocket, picked up his car keys and peered down at Sam. "We'll be back soon, buddy. I'll bring you a doggy bag."

Sam barked once and wagged his tail enthusiastically.

He and Patrice left the room. In the hallway, Patrice resumed her argument. "Besides, abstinence is good for you. It builds character."

"I've got enough character," T.K. told her. "I need more kisses."

She sighed. "We're obviously not going to agree on this."

"Not anytime soon," T.K. assured her.

"Then the bet's still on," she concluded.

"Yes, indeed," he said as they turned the corner and entered the lobby area.

The next morning the cast and crew, sixty-eight people, gathered in the big conference room at the inn.

The director, Mike Whitcomb, a short, stocky African-American in his late thirties who wore his dark brown hair in dreadlocks and had a well-groomed goatee, led the meeting. "The construction crew has finished with the fictional town of Quincy in the Badlands, and tomorrow we will be moving out there in trailers. All of the equipment trucks should be there early in the morning, so we should be able to begin shooting at ten." He regarded T.K. and Patrice, who were sitting up front side by side. "We'll be starting with the love scene. Let's get that out of the way, shall we?"

Patrice was dumbfounded. She was aware that the director chose which scene to shoot based on lighting and based on weather conditions, and it was always his prerogative, but why the love scene first? It wasn't as if they would be out in inclement weather. According to the script, it would take place in a cabin in the fictional black township of Quincy.

She sighed, hoping T.K., sitting beside her, was just as uncomfortable shooting the love scenes so early in filming.

It turned out, he was. "Mike, what's your reasoning on shooting the love scene first? I'm sure Patrice and I would both feel more relaxed if it came later on down the line."

"It's warm now," Mike explained. "The weather in these parts drops ten degrees or more with each successive month. As you know, there is no heating on the makeshift sets they threw up to represent the township of

Quincy." Patrice couldn't believe Mike Whitcomb was blushing. "You and Patrice will be quite scantily clad for the scenes. I don't want my stars catching cold."

Everybody laughed except T.K. and Patrice, who looked at one another and smiled regretfully. "Well, you tried," Patrice whispered to T.K., indicating that she was grateful for his chivalrous efforts.

Soon after, the meeting broke up, and the two of them went to breakfast, which they'd earlier skipped. Over bagels and coffee in the inn's dining room, T.K. took her hand in his. Their eyes met. "I had them put your trailer next to mine. I hope you don't think that was presumptuous of me. I want you near so I can look out for you. The area we'll be going to is about 40 miles west of here. They call it the Badlands, but what they are is wasteland, arid, rocky, hell to hike on and ride on. It's pretty isolated, so if somebody has an accident, it's going to take some maneuvering to get them out of there and to help. Of course, they have so-called experts, horse wranglers and other stunt coordinators who're supposed to make the stunts safe for everybody, but I've done thirty films and I know accidents happen."

Patrice was touched by his concern. "I'll be all right. Don't worry about me. But it's nice to know you care. By the way, what happened to Mark? I thought he'd be at the meeting."

"He only came yesterday to smooth things over with local officials. He's gone home."

T.K.'s brown eyes swept over her face. He wanted to

tell her he cared about her. Already his mind was in a near panic because tomorrow they were going to have to enact a love scene that, when he'd read it, had made him wonder how he would ever get through it without embarrassing himself. Could he be detached enough tomorrow to hide the fact that even sitting across from her at a table in a dining room he was getting aroused? God, help him.

He'd worked with Mike on several movies, though. If Mike saw that he was getting into trouble, he would call "Cut!" and allow him time to fix the problem.

Patrice smiled at him. "This will be my first love scene in a film," she said shyly. "I might need your help to get through it."

You might need my help? T.K. thought ruefully. *I'm going to need a minor miracle in order to get through that scene tomorrow.*

He smiled gently and said while squeezing her hand reassuringly, "Relax, there's nothing to it."

"Seriously?" she innocently asked.

"Sure, it'll be over before you know it. Believe me, after so many starts and stops with all the technical stuff, you'll be bored out of your mind before it's over."

"I want a closed set as much as we can get it!" yelled Mike the following morning. "Only those essential to the shoot need to remain."

Patrice, standing beside T.K. on the set that was designed to look like the bedroom of a rustic nineteenth-century cabin, was relieved. She watched as thirty people left the area. She was in costume. Extensions gave her a head full of curls. Underneath the frilly red dress, she wore a corset that was cutting off her breath. She was almost eager for T.K. to rip it off her. The dastardly thing had so many fasteners on it that there would be no ripping, though. He would have to carefully remove it, as the script dictated.

When Mike was pleased that he had a closed set, he gestured to T.K. and Patrice. "All right, guys. Let's get this show on the road."

Patrice smiled up at T.K. He looked handsome in his marshal's uniform of jeans, a black denim shirt with Western buttons, his silver badge on his left breast pocket and boots. They'd given him a handlebar mustache that looked authentic, and it gave him a tough, utterly masculine appearance.

There were a few words of dialogue as they entered the bedroom. As Bella, Patrice looked up at T.K., as Bass, and said, "After everything I've been through, I couldn't stand it if you didn't treat me kindly." She looked beseechingly up at him. Bass's expression was tender. In it, she saw that he didn't regard her as a used woman but something precious.

"I'll treat you like the angel you are," he said in his rough yet tender voice. Then they kissed, and Bella held her head back so that he could kiss the lovely lines of her throat.

Patrice's bosom was pushed up to such an extent by

the tight corset that she was afraid her breasts would spill out of it. She concentrated. When T.K.'s hands went to her chest, she told herself, *I'm Bella. Be Bella. She isn't timid. She knows how to please a man and is bold enough to show a man how to please her.*

Mike allowed them to move through the script on their own, not saying a thing. It was quiet on the set. In the make-believe bedroom, Bass and Bella were kissing tenderly as if both of them were wounded souls and had to be nurtured. He rained kisses down her throat, ending with his lips on the crevice where her breasts came together in the corset.

Patrice trembled with pleasure. Bella aside, she was turned on by T.K. Bass removed Bella's corset and her breasts, perfect, heavy and hard-tipped, fell into his big hands. For a moment, T.K. forgot the role he was playing, and he saw only Patrice. He felt as if he were doing something bad, when she hadn't given him permission to touch her so intimately. Still, that thought didn't stop the erection that followed.

Bella unbuttoned Bass's shirt and ran her hands over his smooth, muscular chest. Patrice's hands touched T.K.'s hardened nipples, and she felt herself growing moist between her legs. *I'm not going to make it,* she thought, panicking. She closed her eyes, and T.K. kissed her. She didn't recall a kiss being in the script at this point.

This was no false kiss either. You could tell when an actor was holding back and not putting himself into it. Oh, God, she couldn't take it. She kissed him back. Then she thought, I get to kiss him! It was like getting a get-out-of-jail-free card. She could kiss him and not be accused of breaking the rules and losing the bet.

She recalled everything from the script, how Bella gestured without speaking, indicating where she wanted Bass to touch her. It was wonderful. In Bella, she'd found free expression. It was almost like making love to T.K. When they mimicked full-on intercourse, there was a thick cloth between them, but they were each naked from the waist up, and their chests were rubbing. What she did for art! They screamed in ecstasy, and it was over. They fell onto the bed, exhausted but satisfied.

Mike yelled, "Cut!"

Patrice grabbed a blanket and wrapped it around her. T.K. remained covered by the sheet, not moving for fear it would be quite apparent that the scene had been a difficult one for him. He prided himself on his control, but this time he'd lost it.

"Please tell me you got that in one take," he said to Mike.

Mike laughed shortly. "All I need now is a cigarette."

Patrice was mortified. Had it been that erotic? She thought she had gone someplace else for a minute there, that she had been Bella instead of herself. She was sure that T.K. had lost himself in the scene, too.

"I'm just joking," Mike assured them. "The scene went beautifully. I'll take a look at the rushes and let you know if we need a reshoot, but I sincerely don't think so. Get ready for the canyon scene."

Patrice went and sat on the side of the bed. She wasn't ignorant. She knew why T.K. hadn't moved yet. "Nothing to it, huh?" she whispered accusingly. "That was not a piece of cake. I could have made love to you right then and there. I was totally into you." She rose, piercing him with a stare. "No wonder actors fall in love on location."

With an exasperated huff, she stormed off the set.

T.K. sat there a few more minutes and contemplated the scene. She wouldn't believe him if he told her he'd never before gotten an erection during a love scene. It was all Mike's fault. Usually the director was yelling, "No, that wasn't right, do it this way," or, "Cut," making the scene mundane. Mike had allowed them to play out the scene and had remained silent. The one time T.K. would have welcomed constructive criticism from his director he hadn't gotten it. Patrice was going to think he was a horn dog.

Chapter 8

An hour later they were in costumes for the chase scene. T.K. was in his marshal's uniform, and unfortunately, it was a dress complete with a bustle and corset for Patrice. In this scene, they were running from a lynch mob across the Badlands. The horse wranglers hadn't appeared yet with their mounts, so they were standing outside arguing about the love scene. "Have you no shame?" Patrice asked, skewering him with her eyes. "You kissed me for real! That was *not* acting."

T.K. shrugged. "You kissed me back, so technically I won the bet."

"I didn't kiss you back," Patrice denied. "You said that I had to kiss you when it wasn't in the line of duty. I kissed you during a scene that was being filmed. So I didn't break any rules."

"Tell the truth and shame the devil," T.K. said with a laugh. "I know when I'm being kissed, and you kissed the hell out of me!"

Patrice gave him a calculated smile. "Prove it!"

But before T.K. could respond, members of the cast and crew flooded the street around them in the fictional town of Quincy. They fell silent. There was no use in making a spectacle of themselves. Patrice let him know with a cutting glance that she wasn't finished with him yet though. The horse wranglers brought their mounts, and they climbed onto their backs. It was time to work.

The cinematographer sat on the back of a truck in a specially made seat that would allow him to move around and position himself at different angles from which he could shoot the action, and Mike was on the back of another truck in a similar seat. He shouted, "Action!" and watched as his actors galloped out of town into the Badlands.

Patrice had the first line. Bella grinned at Bass as they fled. "I'm beginning to think knowing you is liable to get me killed!"

Six men on horseback chased them, shooting bullets that whizzed by their heads, barely missing them, but Bella and Bass seemed to be having the time of their lives.

As the day progressed, Patrice found herself actually tiring of being on a horse. While the actors weren't allowed to do anything that would jeopardize their lives, there was a great need to get as many shots as possible of them atop their mounts. It was dusk before Mike called it a day, and by that time, Patrice's inner thigh muscles and her butt were sore.

The horse wranglers came and collected the horses, and she and T.K. walked slowly back to their trailers. "Still want to be a movie star?" he joked.

Patrice wanted to rub her pained bottom but refrained. "I wouldn't trade it for anything else," she said with forced enthusiasm.

T.K. laughed. "Don't tell me you're not sore. I'm aching in places I didn't know I had."

"I would pay you to massage my butt for me," Patrice joked.

"I would pay you to let me," T.K. returned.

Laughing, Patrice turned to look up into his smiling face. "Who do you think I am, Bella?"

T.K. threw his head back in laughter. He pulled her into the crook of his arm as they made their way to the area where the cast's trailers were parked. Patrice momentarily laid her head on his shoulder, and then she placed her arm about his waist. He was dirty and sweaty, just like she was, but he smelled heavenly to her.

After a quick shower and change in their respective trailers, they met at the caterer's tent where many of the cast and crew were enjoying dinner. They sat at a table with four other actors. One of them, Ted Knowles, portrayed Bass's nemesis, Jesse Beaumont, a crooked sheriff who was bent on revenge because he didn't believe Bass, a lawman and a bounty hunter, should be allowed to bring in white outlaws and collect the bounties. Bass was so good at collecting bounties that he'd become quite well-off from it. This further incensed Ted Knowles' character, and he'd falsely accused Bass of gunning a man down in cold blood, and that's why a posse was after him. Bella was wanted for aiding and abetting Bass.

"I hear that love scene was hot," Ted joked as soon as Patrice and T.K. sat down.

Lara Miller, a brunette who portrayed a prostitute who worked at the brothel where Bella worked, poked Ted in the side with her elbow. "You're just jealous you weren't in it with Patrice." She winked at Patrice.

Ted's tanned cheeks darkened in a noticeable blush. He smiled at Patrice, though, and said, "I'm sorry you had to have your first love scene with a guy as ugly as T.K.

"The acting gods should have mercy on you and give you someone like me next time."

He said this self-deprecatingly because no one would say Ted Knowles was handsome. He was a big, rugged-looking guy in his late thirties with dark hair that was thinning on top. His eyes were small, and his nose was large. He had thin lips and not much of a chin. He was a character actor who was known for portraying villains the audience loved to hate. He took pride in that. But as villainous as his characters were he was just as sweet in real life. He was the sort of actor other actors loved working with.

"We can't all be as handsome as you are," T.K. said

with sincerity. "If I were a woman I'd marry you in a second." And he rose and kissed Ted on the bald spot on the top of his head.

"Aw, now, quit it," said Ted wiping the spot where T.K. had kissed him as though he were disgusted. "My wife doesn't take kindly to anybody else kissing my bald spot."

Patrice got up and kissed it, too.

"Well, I don't have to tell her everything," said Ted.

They all laughed and continued eating.

The cast and crew lived in trailers during the week, T.K.'s being the most luxurious among them. On weekends, they went to Casper, the closest city to them, looking for entertainment. When August ended, September arrived with a twelve-degree drop in the temperature: the lower seventies during the day and the lower forties at night.

During the week, after filming had wrapped, the cast and crew ate dinner together underneath the caterer's tent and then retired to their trailers to chat, watch movies, play cards or amuse themselves in some other way. Patrice noticed that since they had begun work on the film a few couples had formed among the cast and crew. She suspected that some thought she and T.K. were a couple, too; however, even though they'd exchanged keys to their trailers she hadn't succumbed to him yet.

They would take Sam on long walks in the evening, and T.K. and Sam would see her to the door of her trailer.

There, she would give him a warm hug and say good-night.

In her bed, though, she would burn for him. She didn't know how he was coping, but their bet was beginning to wear on her nerves.

By October, when the daylight hours saw temperatures in the lower fifties, exacerbated by bitter winds coming off the plains and dipping into the lower thirties at night, Patrice's mood turned as dark as the weather. Cast and crew were now walking around outside bundled up and trying their best to stay warm. By November, when temperatures could drop to twenty degrees at night, Patrice felt lonelier and lonelier in her trailer during the long nights.

Everyone flew home for Thanksgiving, and Patrice was happy to be in the bosom of her family in Albuquerque where they observed all the long-held traditions of the holiday. T.K. went to his parents' home in Beverly Hills. Aisha had given birth to a healthy baby girl two weeks earlier and named her Mira. The doctor gently swabbed the inside the baby's mouth for the DNA test and was able to determine that Mira was indeed Malcolm's child. The McKennas celebrated. And T.K. wondered what Aisha's next move would be now that it had been proven she was telling the truth.

He didn't have to wait long because shortly after Thanksgiving dinner, she asked to speak with him privately, and he found himself in his father's study, standing a few feet from the new mother who was dressed rather inappropriately in a blouse that was too tight and a skirt that was too short. He knew she had money to buy clothes that fit because he provided her with a generous clothing allowance.

She paced while he calmly sat on the corner of his dad's desk. From time to time, she would look at him as if she were uncertain how to begin. She had a nervous habit of twirling her long, black extensions around her manicured fingers and pouting.

Suddenly she stopped pacing and frowning and blurted, "Now that you know Mira's Malcolm's, what are you prepared to do to keep her in the family?"

Taken aback, T.K. stood up. "What do you mean by that?" Her tone had been belligerent, as though she were issuing a threat, not simply asking a question.

She smiled demurely and walked slowly toward him. "I've seen the way you look at me. I think that as Malcolm's brother you should step up and take his place. I'd make a good wife."

T.K.'s first impulse was to laugh. Then he got so angry that he wanted to scream at her for making such a ridiculous suggestion. However, he did neither. It was obvious the woman was either delusional or a worse schemer than he'd thought she was.

He kept his tone low as he looked her in the eyes and said, "I don't know what you mean by 'the way I look at you' because I've never looked at you in any particular way. You're my brother's baby's mother. I would never consider marrying you."

Aisha was crestfallen. Her lower lip began trembling, and her eyes filled with tears.

"I'm not good enough for you?"

T.K. didn't want to hurt her feelings further. She had given birth two weeks ago. She was still healing. She might be suffering from postpartum depression for all he knew. "It's not that, Aisha," he said kindly. "The fact is I'm involved with someone else. Even if I weren't, it's distasteful for me to consider making love to a woman who has made love to and created a life with my brother. That would be dishonoring his memory. I loved Malcolm. *You* loved Malcolm. Let us come to some kind of agreement so that Mira will grow up knowing who her father was and being close to his family. I'm prepared to support you and Mira for the rest of your lives. But my marrying you is out of the question."

Aisha's tears stopped falling as suddenly as they had appeared. She turned narrowed, hate-filled eyes on him and spoke between clenched teeth. "Marry me or I'll take Mira and disappear. You'll never see her again."

T.K. sighed and crossed his arms over his chest. He gave her a level stare. "Aisha, if that's what you want to do, you should do it. But I don't think that's what you want to do. You have no discernible skills. The only job you've ever had was as a waitress in a diner in East L.A."

Her mouth fell open in shock. "You've been checking up on me?"

"I don't let just anyone move in with my parents,"

T.K. told her. "You have been a rap groupie in hopes that someone would cast you in a rap video. You latched on to Malcolm because he was kind to you. That was Malcolm. He had a good heart. You were aware of his mental disability, and you took advantage of it. Let's not hold anything back, if that's how you want to carry on this conversation. You are a liar, and I wouldn't be surprised if you were a thief as well. Malcolm's bank accounts were rapidly dwindling while he was with you. You no longer had access after his death, which I'm sure helped you to decide to accept my offer to take care of you until the baby was born. Have I said enough, or would you like me to go on?"

Tears once again sprang to her eyes. "I can't take care of a baby. I'm twenty-six, and my life is over!" She put a hand over her still-puffy belly. "I'm out of shape. No man is going to want me like this. I have nowhere to go. And who's going to want me when I'm saddled with a baby, anyway?"

"I told you that I'll support you and Mira," T.K. reiterated.

For a split second, T.K. noted, her eyes took on an avaricious glint. Then, almost instantly, they were back to looking downcast. "How would you support us?" she asked timidly.

"I would buy you a house in or near L.A. and give you a monthly stipend," said T.K. generously.

He knew that by doing that he would never get rid of Aisha. However, to have Mira in his life, his brother's only child, he would gladly do it. Already he loved the infant. From the moment he'd held her in his arms, it had felt as if he had a small part of Malcolm back.

"If you wanted to go to college, I would pay for it," he added.

"College? Why would I want to go to college?" asked Aisha as if it were a preposterous idea.

"To improve yourself, to set a good example for Mira, to increase your net worth," said T.K. "I'm not made of money, Aisha. After I buy the house, I'll be able to give you fifty thousand a year to live on. If you want more luxuries, you'll have to go to work and buy them yourself."

"But what about Mira?" asked Aisha. "Will you make her go to work and earn whatever luxuries she might want later on?"

"Mira's education will be taken care of," was all T.K. said. He had no intention of spoiling Mira with things. He wouldn't be doing her any favors, just helping to turn her into someone like her greedy mother.

"I'll think about it," Aisha said, and flounced from the room, twirling her hair as she went. T.K. watched her go, wishing he were anywhere but there. To think that she wanted him to marry her! She had plenty of gall.

He went to the phone on his father's desk and rang his lawyer, Saul Abraham. Saul answered on the third ring. He explained to Saul what had just happened and asked him to find out what, if any, rights he or his parents had to custody of his niece. Saul promised to get back to him as soon as possible.

As he left the study, he yearned for Patrice. He couldn't wait to get back to Wyoming tomorrow, even if they *would* be filming in the snow.

When he and Sam left Los Angeles, flying this time for convenience, it had been an almost balmy sixty-two degrees. When they touched down in Wyoming, it was eighteen degrees. Sam didn't even protest when he put on his doggy coat before leaving the terminal.

Someone from the crew picked him up at Casper/Natrona County International Airport and drove him out to the site where the RVs were parked. After leaving Sam at his trailer, he knocked on Patrice's door.

There was no answer.

He had not thought to ask the crew member if she was back yet. He looked around him. No one was out in this weather. The wind was bitingly cold, and the sound was like a banshee's wail. What was more is that since the sun had gone down the temperature had continued to drop rapidly. She couldn't be out in this weather.

He jogged back over to his trailer and was greeted at the door by Patrice. She grinned and pulled him inside. "Why didn't you check in the bedroom when you came in?" She was warm and toasty he discovered as he pulled her into his arms. She hugged him tightly then began helping him out of his bulky hooded coat.

"I had your key. I didn't mean to fall asleep," she

told him. "Sam woke me. I knew you couldn't be far so I came into the living room to wait for you. How are you?"

T.K. was so happy to see her that he forgot about the bet and kissed her. She kissed him back. "I missed you so much," she cried when he finally let her up for air. Her lovely brown eyes bored into his, and he saw that she had indeed missed him. He kissed her again and again. He had months of kisses to make up for.

When they parted this time, he asked, "What made you give in?"

She reached up and held his face between her hands. "Being with my family," she said softly, "made me miss you more. Oh, I had a great time cooking Thanksgiving dinner with my mom and watching the game on TV. It was wonderful being with them. My heart was filled with love for them, but there was one key player missing— you." She tried to read in his eyes how her statement had affected him. She only saw his desire for her in them. She gently kissed his lips. "I really like you, Trevor."

An indescribable feeling of happiness came over T.K. At last, he could tell her how he felt about her without worrying about that damn bet. Why had he ever come up with such a stupid idea in the first place? "I couldn't wait to get back to you, either, Patty Cakes," he told her, gazing down at her as though he could devour her whole.

"Oh, my God, not a nickname," exclaimed Patrice,

but the sheer joy on her face belied her irritation. "Just kiss me!"

He did, and he kept on kissing her all the way back to his bedroom where he undressed her and then undressed himself, and they began to create their own love scene without a script in sight.

Chapter 9

"Mmm, you smell good," said T.K. as he kissed her neck and worked his way down her naked body. Her back was pressed against the bedroom wall. His hands cupped her hips as he knelt and licked her flat belly. Patrice held on to his powerful shoulders to maintain her balance. She felt weak with desire, her nipples were hard and she was wet and throbbing between her legs.

She made an attempt at conversation to try to quell the mad beating of her heart. "I soaked in your tub while I was waiting."

From his kneeling position, he looked up at her and smiled. "So you were planning on seducing me?"

She quivered. "The thought had crossed my mind. I hope you've got condoms, or I'm going to be highly upset we have to stop," she told him.

T.K. laughed and rose. He picked her up and carried her to the bed. "I was optimistic. There are a few dozen in the nightstand drawer."

Patrice let out a longing-filled sigh as he placed her on the bed and knelt over her.

She drew him down and kissed him, her back arching upward. T.K. was already erect and steadily growing harder. He lowered his body onto hers, keeping his full weight off her with his strong arms. The urge to plunge into her was unbearably sweet. He didn't want to dwell on it for fear he'd embarrass himself by ejaculating early.

But what else could he do when her delicious body was pressed against his and she was writhing so temptingly beneath him? He felt her sex against him. It was so warm and inviting. The tip of his penis was at the opening, and she was shivering with need, almost panting, and he did what any red-blooded male would do: he took the plunge. Ah, she was tight. He felt her eager sex contract as if the lips of her vagina were her lips and she wanted to devour him. He couldn't take it. He pushed, crying, "Oh, God, you feel good!"

She cried out too, and then they were thrusting. She gave herself joyfully, as though a dam that was holding back her passion had suddenly broken and all of it was pouring forth for him. He rode her hard, his thrusts going deeper with each push and the momentum building. She screamed as a powerful orgasm ripped through her. At the sound of her release, he came to his senses and pulled out. His seed spilled onto her belly. He fell on top of her, half ashamed of himself for not being strong enough to resist her long enough to put on a condom.

His body convulsed. Patrice was kissing his chest. He rolled over onto his back, thinking his bulk was probably smothering her. Up on his elbow, he peered into her face. "I'm sorry. That was worse than a teenage boy doing it with his girlfriend for the first time in the backseat of his car."

"I don't know what you're talking about," Patrice told him, running a finger along his jaw. "It was intense. I loved it."

He gratefully rained kisses on her face.

"But I think I'll be in charge of the condoms from now on," she added with a smile.

He laughed shortly. "Yes, ma'am. Maybe you ought to be. I forgot they existed for a moment there."

"How about we shower together and see where that leads us," Patrice proposed.

He was down with that and got up and pulled her to her feet. He paused when he heard a scratching at the door. Sam wanted to be let into the bedroom.

"I'll be right back," he said. "Go ahead and start without me."

Patrice went to the bathroom, and he went to open the door. Sam ran straight to Patrice. T.K. had a hard time corralling the dog and ushering him back out to the living room. "I think he missed you," he said.

Patrice took a moment to rub Sam under the chin.

"I'm really sorry, boy, but it would freak me out if you stayed."

T.K. grabbed Sam by the collar, and Sam allowed him to lead him outside. "You're embarrassing me," he whispered. "Can't you see I've finally got her where I want her? Don't ruin this for me."

Sam whined. T.K. led him to the kitchen and bribed him with his favorite kibble. "Just a little bit," he said as he poured it into Sam's food bowl. "I'll take you for a short walk later on."

Sam whined again when the wind whistled. T.K. laughed. "Yeah, I know it's cold outside, but you still need to go out later."

He left Sam enjoying his snack in the kitchen and hurried back to Patrice, who was already soaping her body by the time he entered the bathroom. He watched her for a moment. She was beautiful to him. She wasn't beautiful in the Hollywood sense of the word. She didn't have perfect features, and her breasts, although heavenly to him, hadn't been augmented to inhuman proportions. She was healthy and vibrant, and the combination of her warm brown skin, toned and muscular body, wide-spaced brown eyes, high cheekbones, pert nose, full lips and raven's-wing hair was like an aphrodisiac to him. She was a real woman, and after so many women who were not real walking in and out of his life for the past eighteen years, he could now appreciate a real woman.

Patrice caught him watching her and smiled. "Come on in, and tell me about your trip home."

He stepped in and took the washcloth from her, soaped it again and began gently scrubbing her back. "It was wonderful up until Aisha told me I should marry her."

"What?" Patrice laughed. "Whatever possessed her to do that?"

T.K. told her everything. He even told her how Aisha had been trying to insinuate herself into his life ever since Malcolm's death.

"Be careful with that one," Patrice said. "Women like that can be dangerously deluded."

T.K. couldn't agree more, but he didn't want to talk about Aisha anymore. He wanted to put her out of his mind and let the lawyers deal with her.

"How was your trip home? Is everybody in good health? Did you get to ride Billy One Star while you were there?"

She smiled, remembering her visit. "We prepared the traditional Thanksgiving meal with a Southwestern flavor."

"Then I suppose there were hot peppers in every dish, even the dessert," T.K. said.

Patrice laughed. "There were some spicy dishes, but two members of the family were not partaking as often as they used to. Keira and Nina are expecting. Momma and Daddy are beside themselves with joy—two grandchildren!"

"Our families have had a banner year for babies," T.K. said. "First Mira, and now two more are on the way."

They were finished showering, so he reached up and

turned off the spray. He grabbed a big, clean soft bath towel from the rack next to the stall and draped it around Patrice's shoulders. Peering into her eyes, he asked, "Do you like babies?"

Patrice was a little taken aback by the question. Was he talking about babies because they had just been discussing new additions to their families? Or could he be asking her if she liked them because he personally wanted to know if she wanted babies of her own?

"Who doesn't like babies?" she asked.

T.K. could think of a few people who didn't. Edina had said she would never bear a child and risk losing her figure. Aisha apparently was willing to barter her child for money. "Not all women like children," he said.

The expression in his eyes told her that he was saddened by this knowledge. She grasped him by the arm and made him look at her. "I'm not one of them. I love babies. Why do you ask?"

He told her about his request to Saul Abraham. "If Aisha continues to threaten to take Mira and disappear, we'll try to get custody of her. If we do, I would be the one to raise her. I want to be with you, Patty. I wondered if you would want to be with me if I came with a baby."

Patrice took the towel, placed it behind his neck and pulled him down for a kiss. When she broke off the kiss, she smiled at him. "I adore you, and I'll adore her, too."

After they dried off, T.K. led her back to his bedroom

where he asked her to sit on the bed while he took care of a few things. Intrigued, Patrice asked him what things. He gave her an enigmatic smile and told her to be patient.

He left the room. A couple minutes later, Patrice heard Maxwell's gorgeous tenor on the sound system. She got a condom out of the nightstand drawer, held it in the palm of her hand and then climbed into bed and covered herself with the top sheet. She was sitting in bed with her knees drawn up when he returned with a bottle of champagne and two wine glasses.

He sat on the side of the bed, opened the champagne, carefully filled the two glasses and handed her one. Turning around, he touched his glass lightly to hers. "To the victor go the spoils."

Patrice laughed because she knew exactly to what he was referring. He'd won the bet; therefore, he was the victor, and she was the spoils. He'd already had her. "I didn't want to take your precious Camaro and make you cry," she said in her defense.

"You can have it," he told her. "You can paint it pink for all I care. I've got you, and I'm victorious."

She leaned over and kissed him lightly on the lips. "How sweet, but I'll keep my Jeep, thanks."

T.K., who was used to giving his lovers extravagant gifts, was a bit surprised by her refusal. "Then you can pick out any car you would like to have."

Patrice drank some of her champagne and eyed him. "I

don't need two cars. I like my Jeep. I don't need anything else."

"Well, then how about jewelry?" He'd noticed she didn't wear a lot of jewelry. Maybe she didn't want to buy it for herself. Right now she was only wearing a pair of gold hoop earrings—and not the huge hoops, either, but something small and tasteful.

He frowned. "You don't want a flashy car, and you don't appear to be into jewelry. You dress nicely, but you're not a clotheshorse. What *do* you like?"

"Think about it a moment, and get back to me," Patrice told him, this time giving *him* an enigmatic smile. She sipped her champagne while T.K. thought about their time together. He even went back as far as the first conversation he'd had with anyone about her, and that had been Mark when Mark had phoned him and told him that Patrice had just participated in a rodeo.

"Oh, my God," he said when the realization struck him. "You're a simple girl in Hollywood. They're going to eat you alive."

Patrice laughed. "You're wrong. I'm a *smart,* simple girl in Hollywood. Now, tell me what I like, Trevor."

He put his champagne glass down, took hers and set it next to his on the nightstand, then drew her into his arms. They lay comfortably on the bed, wrapped together in the top sheet. "You like riding horses. You like making your surroundings beautiful. You spend a lot of time on your home. You like having loved ones around you, and you like feeding them. You like driving, too. If you have the time, you'd rather drive than fly to a destination because you like the feel of the road."

She snuggled up to him. "Bravo, you get me."

"I'll buy you a ranch, and you can pick out all the horses you like," T.K. said.

Patrice climbed on top of him. "Why don't I just ride *you?*" She scooted down and licked him from the hollow of his throat to below his navel. T.K.'s penis grew hard fast.

Patrice licked him along the underside and paused at the tip. He was mesmerized. Her beautiful mouth on him sent blood rushing to his member.

As much as he loved the feel of her mouth on him, though, he wanted her pleasure even more. He stopped her just as she was about to take him fully into her mouth.

"Not yet, baby. I want to enjoy you first," he told her, and with muscles flexing, he lifted her and laid her on the bed on her back.

What he'd only imagined for months he now did to her. He took his time tonguing her nipples, which were sweet and ripe, the sensation unbelievably satisfying. He was so hard he was literally in pain. Patrice was enjoying it, too. She arched her back with her sex thrust toward him as if she was begging him to take her. He held on to his control, though.

Then his gaze rested on her sex—her wet, swollen sex. He lowered his head and feasted. Patrice couldn't hold back a little yelp that assured him he was doing something right. He was gentle but thorough, only stopping after her body lay quivering on the bed. Then he spied the condom lying on the bed, she must have gotten it while he'd been getting the champagne. He got it and put it on. He spread her legs and none too gently thrust into her. Patrice took his roughness by giving it right back to him. She held on to his hips and returned thrust for thrust, looking deeply into his eyes the whole time. She came a few seconds before he did, and the look of extreme pleasure on her face heightened his climax later. He'd never felt this way before. Could it be he'd finally made love to a woman whom he was in love with? He analyzed it. Maybe he hadn't loved Edina at all. He'd held a part of himself aloof from her because he had suspected she wasn't with him out of love. But with Patrice everything was on the table. He was vulnerable with her. His next impulse was to protect himself. But he tossed it out as soon as it had occurred to him. In order to experience love, you had to leave yourself open to being hurt.

They were a bit breathless afterward as they lay in each other's arms.

Patrice sighed with contentment. Her stomach growled. T.K. heard it and laughed.

"I'll get up and scramble some eggs and make you some toast," he said. "I really should have one of the crew go grocery shopping for me."

"I've got food," Patrice said. "We can go to my place."

"Do you know how cold it is out there?"

"It snows in Albuquerque, too. I'm used to it."

"I just want to stay in here with you," T.K. told her.

Her stomach growled again. "I've got roast beef for sandwiches."

"You talked me into it," T.K. said, rising. "I've got to take Sam for a walk anyway."

Patrice got up, went into the bathroom, quickly freshened up and came back out to search for her clothes. She found them tossed aside in the living room, the hallway and the bedroom.

By the time she was dressed, T.K. was also dressed except for his coat. Sam was sitting by the door as if patiently waiting for them.

Patrice zipped up her parka. She was dressed warmly in jeans made of winter-weight denim, an undershirt, a long-sleeved pullover sweater, socks, fur-lined boots and a fur-lined hooded parka. She didn't play with cold weather.

T.K. was more lax in his winter attire. He didn't even have on an undershirt, just a long-sleeved pullover sweater, jeans, thick socks and athletic shoes, with an expensive insulated parka in which he felt warm and toasty.

After pulling on her hood, Patrice went and helped him with his. "Being hair-deprived as you are, you need this," she joked.

He smiled and kissed the tip of her nose. "You look like a cute little Inuit."

They left the RV and immediately felt the urge to turn around and go back inside. The air was bitingly cold on the skin of their faces. The wind was blowing fiercely, and it was snowing.

"I take it back," Patrice said, her breath making white plumes in the icy air. "Albuquerque was never this cold!"

Sam bounded down the steps ahead of them. T.K. had put on his black doggy coat, and he looked kind of like a baby bear in it. T.K. had his leash in his hand but didn't think he needed to use it because he doubted Sam would run off in this weather. The dog was not fond of the cold. He was a real L.A. pooch.

"Hurry up and do your thing, Sam," he urged. He had the blue bag in his coat pocket. It wasn't one of his favorite tasks, but he was a responsible dog owner.

"I wonder if Santa really lives in Wyoming and the claim that he lives in the North Pole is a total fantasy," Patrice joked.

"That guy at the gas station not far from here did resemble St. Nick," said T.K.

Patrice chuckled, remembering the friendly guy with the white beard and hefty build. "Nah, that wasn't Santa. Santa wouldn't own a gas station. A reindeer ranch, maybe."

"How do you know what Santa does in his spare time?"

"Spare time? He has no spare time. He's supervising the elves while they make the toys all year long." She paused when she saw Sam stop by a bush and lift his leg. "We may have some action over there."

A few minutes later, Sam finished, and T.K. went and did his duty, tossing the blue bag into a garbage can.

He left Sam in his trailer and walked with Patrice over to hers. "I don't know what I was thinking when I suggested Wyoming as a location for this movie," he said as he followed her inside. He locked the door behind them. "We could have done it on a Hollywood back lot and faked the snow."

Patrice was pulling off her coat. "That wouldn't have been half as authentic as Wyoming," she disagreed. She put her coat on a nearby chair. T.K. took his off and put it next to hers.

He followed her into the kitchen. "Yeah, but we would have been comfortable."

"Comfort isn't everything. This movie will have some wonderful cinematic moments. The rugged terrain here is worth every penny. Besides, some of my favorite movies were filmed in Wyoming."

"Oh, yeah?" he asked. He washed his hands at the sink, dried them and got the bread from off the counter while Patrice looked in the fridge for the roast beef and other sandwich makings.

"Yeah," said Patrice, her head nearly inside the fridge. "*Shane* and *Close Encounters of the Third Kind,* the first Spielberg movie I ever saw."

"You're so young, I figured your first Spielberg movie would be something from his later years."

"I didn't see it in a theater. I saw it on tape at my friend Beanie's house. We were having a sleepover."

"What's Beanie short for?"

"Benina," said Patrice. "Benina Johnson. She moved away. I haven't seen her in years. These days my best friends are two women I met while at Juilliard, Belana Whitaker and Elle Jones-Corelli."

"Corelli?"

"She married Italian composer Dominic Corelli."

"I know him!"

"You do?" Her arms were full with a package of thin-sliced roast beef, a plastic jar of spicy brown mustard, lettuce, tomatoes and a jar of pickles. She carried everything over to the counter, took a moment to wash and dry her hands and then started making two sandwiches. "How do you know Dominic?"

"I was doing a film near Milan with George Clooney, and George has a house on Lake Como. Dominic has a house—"

"Yeah, I know. That's where the wedding was held."

"Anyway, we all got together and played cards. He's a good player but not nearly as cutthroat as you need to be if you're playing with those guys."

Patrice laughed shortly. "You play cutthroat poker."

"I do," he said, smiling. "Do you play poker?"

"Not well enough to play with you guys, no doubt, but yes, I play. I don't gamble, though, so what's the point?"

"Why don't you gamble?"

"I just have an aversion to wasting money. Growing up, money was tight. There were four of us kids, and sometimes ranching wasn't very lucrative. You have good years and bad years. I guess I learned to be frugal. I'd rather give the money to somebody who can use it rather than gamble it away. That's all."

"I do both," said T.K.

"Yes, I've seen you at charitable events around town," she told him.

"Why is it I never noticed you?"

"Because I was just another young actress clawing her way to the top," said Patrice.

"No," T.K. disagreed, pulling her into his embrace. "You are not just some young actress clawing her way to the top. You're special."

Chapter 10

It was December, and they were at the end of the filming schedule. Patrice felt sad on one hand because she would miss everyone she'd worked with. On the other hand, she was *so* ready to leave the cold of Wyoming behind. People joked that L.A. enjoyed wonderful warm weather because it was so close to the entrance to hell, what with all the sinners who lived there. But she had come to appreciate L.A. more with each passing day. It had been below freezing here every day in December.

Mike had waited for this delightful weather to shoot the gunfight in the snow scene during which Patrice's character, Bella, takes a bullet to the stomach. Of course, no one survived a gut shot in the 1800s. Medicine hadn't been advanced enough back then to work the kinds of miracles that were seen today on a daily basis.

That morning, the wardrobe people dressed her in an emerald-green frilly dress trimmed in black, with long curly extensions hanging down her back, black lace-up ankle boots and a thick black hooded cape. After several starts and stops and, to Patrice, way too much time spent lying in the snow, they got the final scene on film.

In the scene, she was supposed to argue with Ted Knowles' character, Bass Reeves's nemesis, Sheriff Jesse Beaumont. Beaumont had tracked them down, and he'd spotted her in the general store buying more appropriate clothing for the winter weather. He grasped her by the arm and prevented her from leaving. Bella kneed him and fled the store, her only wish to get to Bass and warn him.

She ran out into the street, trying to make it to the livery stable where Bass was bartering with the owner for fresh horses so they could continue their escape unimpeded by exhausted horses. She stopped short when Bass came out of the stable and began walking toward her.

Sheriff Beaumont was right behind her, gun drawn. "Reeves!" he yelled upon seeing Bass. "You stop right there and raise your hands in the air."

Bass, not wanting Bella to get hurt, did what he was told.

"Take off your gun belt and get down on your knees," Beaumont ordered. There was a satisfied smile on his face. He thought he had the upper hand and that he was finally going to see Bass Reeves hang.

"Bass, don't!" Bella shouted, seeing Bass untying the leather straps that held his gun's holster securely against his right thigh.

Beaumont was so hungry for payback that he didn't wait for Bass to loosen the straps and allow his gun belt to fall to the ground. He raised his gun to shoot Bass in cold blood. Bass was concentrating on Bella, so he didn't notice what Beaumont was getting ready to do, but Bella did. She turned and threw herself in front of Bass just as Beaumont fired and the bullet hit her in the midsection.

To Bass's tormented mind, Bella seemed to fall in slow motion.

"No!" Bass shouted and shot Beaumont right between the eyes. The sheriff was dead instantly, and Bass rushed to Bella. It was snowing heavily now, and as he held her head in his lap, her blood stained the snow beneath her. She looked up at him and smiled.

"You were the best time I ever had," she told him.

"You're gonna be okay, Bella. Save your strength," said Bass. A few people were slowly emerging from neighboring buildings and venturing onto the wooden sidewalks. "Somebody get the doc!" he yelled.

A shopkeeper turned and ran in the opposite direction, presumably to fetch a doctor.

Bella's breath was labored now. She continued to smile. "Too late for that," she told Bass. "You'd better go, baby. I'm sure the bastard didn't come alone."

"I won't leave you," Bass stubbornly said. There were tears in his eyes.

"But I'm gonna leave you," Bella said. "Kiss me goodbye."

Bass lowered his head and kissed her, and when he raised his head, her eyes were closed in death.

There was no time for grief though because Bella was right: the bastard had not come alone. Three men stood a few feet behind Bass with guns drawn. One stepped forward and ordered Bass to lay down his gun.

Bass was in no mood to negotiate with crooked lawmen. He rose and faced them, but he didn't relinquish his weapon. With steely eyes, he said, "If you want a fight, you've come to the right man."

He could smell the fear on them. They'd probably signed on with Beaumont because they had figured the colored lawman would be easy prey. Now that Beaumont was lying a few feet away with a bullet in the head, they were not so certain that the job would be a cakewalk.

One of them whispered to the others, "Maybe we ought to get outta here."

Another whispered back, "He's just one man. He can't get all three of us."

"Yeah, but I don't want to be the one he gets. Look at him. He's ready to kill somebody."

Bass was waiting for them to make a move. He was as steady as a rock. Although rage surged through him, he was able to harness it and use it to his benefit.

Two of the men raised their arms and slowly moved away from the one who wanted to remain and fight.

"Toss your guns in the water trough," Bass told them.

They did as they were told.

"Okay, now get the hell outta here!"

They took off running and didn't stop until they reached their horses that they'd left tethered in front of the saloon, where they mounted them and raced out of town.

Bass had his eye on the remaining man the whole time. "Let's get this over with," he told him gruffly.

"You don't scare me, *boy*," said the man. "I've heard about you. They say you killed fourteen outlaws in fair fights. Well, I don't fight fair." With that, he drew his gun, but he wasn't fast enough. Bass shot him through the heart before his finger could pull the trigger. He toppled over, a surprised expression on his florid face.

Bass didn't know it, but the sheriff of the town had watched the entire gunfight. He walked onto the sidewalk adjacent to the spot where Bella still lay in the snow. "You might want to put that firearm away," he said.

Bass, keyed up, turned the gun on him.

The sheriff held up his hands to show he was unarmed. "I'm Sheriff Beaumont. I got a telegraph from the federal judge saying you might be passin' through here and to be on the lookout for you. You're Bass Reeves, a federal marshal, right?"

"How'd you guess?" Bass asked. He knew full well

that besides the four men who followed them there, he and Bella were very likely the only strangers in the little town.

"He sent me a description of you," said the sheriff. "He said you were a tall, tough bastard with a handlebar mustache." He looked with sympathy upon Bella. "I'm sorry about your woman. Do you need help with her?"

"No," Bass told him, going to gather Bella in his arms. "I'll take care of her." As he stood and began walking down the wooden sidewalk, Bella cradled in his arms, the picture faded to black.

"And cut!" shouted Mike. "Congratulations, people! That's a wrap!"

"You cry real pretty," Patrice joked in her Bella voice while still in T.K.'s arms.

"And you die real pretty."

"Where're you taking me?"

"Straight to wardrobe so we can get out of these costumes. Then I'm taking you to my trailer and I'm going to make love to you."

"What about the wrap party?" she asked mischievously.

"We can be a little late," T.K. said.

"People will talk," said Patrice smiling up at him. She was freezing, and the blood pack taped to her stomach was oozing red-colored syrup.

"Get real, Ms. Sutton. People have been talking about us for at least two months now."

She laid her head on his shoulder. "I'm going to miss the mustache."

"Liar," he playfully accused her. "You were horrified it was going to fall off my face every time I kissed you."

"I could imagine I was kissing Tom Selleck."

"Had a thing for him, huh?"

"Only when he was in a Western," said Patrice. "I like my men rough and ready."

"I'll give it to you rough," said T.K. and nuzzled her neck.

They arrived at the RV that housed the costume department. He put her on the top step, and she walked inside and said hello to the two women who immediately began helping her out of the dress.

"When are you heading out, sweetie?" asked one of the women, a sweet-faced grandmotherly type with graying brown hair, warm brown eyes and almond-colored skin.

"Tomorrow morning," said Patrice. She smiled at both of them. "Thank you so much for all you've done."

"It was our pleasure," said the woman's partner, a tall, thin blonde.

"Yes, you were a treat to work with," said the woman with the graying hair. T.K. walked into the room, and the women gasped in unison. "Out," said the grandmotherly woman imperiously. Patrice was down to her corset.

T.K. turned his back to them. "Is this better?"

"It is not," the woman said. "Wait in the hallway, T.K.,

or you'll be sorry." She waved a hat pin threateningly at him.

T.K. took one look at the wickedly long pin and left. "What do you do with that thing?"

"Wouldn't you like to know," said the woman. She smiled at Patrice. "You've got to keep them in line."

Patrice chuckled. "Yes, you do."

"What are you working on next?" asked the other woman, obviously wanting to change the subject. "Got anything lined up?"

"I have a small role in a Johnny Depp film," Patrice told her.

"There are no small roles, only small actors."

"Like that cute little blonde who works on Broadway a lot," her friend quipped.

"Oh, yeah, she's a tiny thing. What's her name?"

"Kristin Chenoweth," Patrice provided the answer. "I loved her in *Pushing Daisies*. Chi McBride was in it, too. Do you know his work?"

The blonde smiled knowingly at her partner.

"What?" asked Patrice, curious to know why the woman had had that wistful expression on her face after she'd mentioned Chi McBride.

"He's a sweetheart," the woman told her confidentially, "so nice and not full of himself like some actors."

Patrice had never worked with him, but that was nice to know.

"Don't tell a certain person I said this," the graying woman said to Patrice, "but Trevor Kennedy is *my* favorite movie star. He's a dear. He treats everybody well, no matter who they are. I've never seen him be unkind to anyone."

Patrice smiled. She knew T.K. was a good man, but it was wonderful to hear people like these ladies say it.

After she'd changed back into her own clothes, she hugged them both. "Take care of yourselves, and I hope to work with you again someday."

By the time T.K. and Patrice arrived at the wrap party, which was being held in the dining room of the inn they'd used at the start of filming, it was in full swing. Although the inn didn't have a live band, they provided the celebrants with music piped in over a sound system and, for those who were brave enough, karaoke. Ted Knowles was on stage singing "I Will Survive" as they walked in.

There was a buffet, and T.K. and Patrice went and filled their plates before sitting at a table near the stage where Lara Miller had waved them over, crying, "Come join us, there're two empty chairs at our table!"

They sat, doffing their coats to reveal casual clothing of jeans, long-sleeved shirts and boots. "He's pretty bad," Patrice said of Ted's singing. She started to playfully shout something encouraging to him but Lara grabbed her by the arm. "Please, don't," she said. "That's his third song. Someone else made the mistake of telling him he sounded good, and he hasn't shut up since."

Patrice smiled at her. "It wasn't you by any chance?"

Lara smiled regretfully. "I learned *my* lesson."

Patrice and T.K. ate their meals, entertained the entire time by Ted, who was now being intermittently booed. T.K. put down his fork and rose. "Someone's got to end this madness."

He reached down for Patrice's hand. "Come on."

Patrice laughed. "You're on your own, big guy."

"Chicken?" asked T.K., laughter evident in his eyes.

Patrice grudgingly stood up, "All right, but no disco." While she was at Juilliard, she'd taken voice lessons and dance lessons with the goal of becoming a well-rounded actor.

However, she would never compare her singing to Elle's or her dancing to Belana's. They were devoted to their disciplines as she was devoted to hers, and it showed.

So it was with a bit of trepidation that she went onstage with T.K.

Ted took being kicked to the curb with his usual sense of humor. "Good luck," he told them as he walked off the stage. "This crowd's hard to please."

Patrice and T.K. perused the song list for a moment and decided on "Ain't No Mountain High Enough." When the music began, they stood onstage back to back, microphones held in their hands at the ready.

The music started and T.K., taking Marvin Gaye's part, turned around and sang to Patrice. They stood close, arms around one another's waists.

Patrice gazed up at him the way Tammi Terrell used

to gaze up at Marvin Gaye, and she sang with as much sincerity. She was pleasantly surprised that T.K. could carry a tune. He was no Marvin, but who was? He was getting into it, too, looking at her as if she were the most desirable creature in the world when he pledged to be there no matter what. Patrice let go and belted out the chorus, and T.K. met the challenge, matching her enthusiasm.

When they finished, they got a standing ovation.

Ted yelled from the back, "When's the wedding?"

Everybody got a good laugh out of that one. T.K., looking into Patrice's upturned face, thought the idea had merit. What would it be like to share his life with Patrice? The past four months had been among the happiest he'd ever spent, entirely owing to her. Was love enough to sustain a marriage in Hollywood?

He'd seen so many marriages between actors fail. There were a few that survived until the couples had been parted in death. Foremost in his mind were Ruby Dee and Ossie Davis and Paul Newman and Joanne Woodward. All were actors. All remained devoted to one another for more than fifty years. Could he and Patrice have a marriage that stood the test of time?

Patrice was smiling strangely at him. He smiled warmly. "Sorry, I was lost in thought."

They walked down the steps of the stage, allowing an actress to take it. T.K. took Patrice's hand. "Can we get out of here?"

Patrice was agreeable. She hadn't fully recovered

from lying in the snow during their last scene together and wanted nothing more than a long soak in a deep tub of hot water. Before coming here, they had checked into T.K.'s suite. That's where they'd left Sam, who was probably bored by now. "Yeah, let's go," she said.

They went back to the table where Lara and Ted were sitting. Patrice collected her shoulder bag and they said their farewells. Some of the people in this room they might never work with again; however, many of them they would see again during the course of their careers. Hollywood, while seemingly big to outsiders, was really made up of a rather small community of like-minded individuals.

Holding hands, they left the dining room.

Alone with Patrice in the corridor, T.K. paused to grasp her face between his hands and kiss her lips. Lifting his mouth from hers, he said, "What do you think of marriage?"

Patrice's eyes widened. T.K. smiled. He hoped he hadn't panicked the poor girl.

"I'm not asking you. I only wanted to know your opinion on the whole institution. Are you for it or against it?"

He took her hand again and they continued walking toward the lobby, which was pretty deserted at this time of night, ten-thirty. They would have to cross it to get to his suite.

"I would definitely prefer marriage over single parenthood," Patrice said. "Not so much because I care what society thinks of me but rather what my parents think of me. They've had a long, happy marriage."

"So have mine," T.K. said contemplatively. Earlier he had held two Hollywood marriages in high esteem, forgetting about his own parents'. Patrice helped him to keep his feet on the ground. That's another reason he admired her. She was down-to-earth and valued family, plus she had high ideals. She wasn't afraid to say her parents' opinion of her mattered.

"So you believe that two people can remain devoted to one another for the rest of their lives?"

Patrice gave him a puzzled look. "Of course I do. What are you getting at, Trevor?"

He loved it when she called him Trevor.

"I'm wondering how long I should wait before asking you to marry me," he told her, making her stop in her tracks. He went on, not noticing that she was stunned. He stopped walking too, though, and peered into her eyes. "I love you, and to be honest, I don't think I've ever been in love before. I was always bent on watching out for T. K. McKenna's interests. I realize now that's the reason I was convinced that Edina wasn't with me out of love. She gave me no outward evidence of her infidelity until the end, yet I was still sure that she couldn't love me. She might have loved T. K. McKenna but not me."

Her mind reeling from his admission of love, Patrice nonetheless had to ask, "Why do you keep referring to yourself in that way?"

"Because T. K. McKenna is not me. I'm Trevor. T.K.

is a Hollywood fabrication. With you, I feel like I can be Trevor, and you wouldn't miss T.K. at all. You tend to reject me when I'm being T.K. You turned down my gifts. I'm incapable of impressing you with being one of the biggest box-office draws in the world because you don't care about that. All you care about is whether or not I'm a good actor—and that I'm a good person."

"That's the only thing that lasts in this business," Patrice agreed. "You may not always be on top, but you can still turn in fine performances. It's so sad when aging actors keep trying to be the action hero because that's all they know. You're more than that. You're a fine actor."

He laughed. "I thank you for that, but you know my opinion of acting. It's just a job. However, for you, I will expand my repertoire to more character roles and stop trying to save the world in every one of my films. Now, can we get back on the subject of marriage? Is it too soon to ask you, or should we wait a few months? Are you a traditionalist? Should I meet your parents before thinking of asking you?"

They'd arrived at his suite. He unlocked the door and allowed her to precede him inside. Sam came running to greet them.

Patrice knelt and rubbed his shaggy head. She was avoiding answering T.K.'s questions because she was trembling inside with excitement. She loved him. But marriage was a huge step. He had been a bachelor for a relatively long time. Did he really know what marriage entailed? The compromises one had to make? Not that she was an authority, but she did know that marrying someone was not like living with them. Marriage required faith in the relationship—faith in the person you married. It meant that no matter what that you would stand by them. She didn't want to get married and get divorced a year later. When she married, she wanted it to last.

She rose and faced T.K. Looking into his eyes, his expression expectant, she said, "Sometimes I forget how decisive you can be. When you want something, you go after it with no notion whatsoever that you might fail in the pursuit." She smiled. "That's admirable. Really, it is. But know this—when I get married I want it to last. Don't ever propose to me if you're not prepared to love me for the rest of your life. That's a deal breaker. And to answer your other question, yes, I'd like you to meet my parents before you decide if I'm the woman for you. My family comes with me—just like your family comes with you. I'm not saying that I wouldn't marry you if they didn't like you. Then I would have to tell them I don't need their approval to marry the man I love."

T.K. grinned, and then he kissed her long and hard. She made him believe that love could last forever. He raised his head. "Then take me home to meet your parents."

Chapter 11

Patrice and T.K. got back to Los Angeles on December 20. They had driven T.K.'s SUV, taking turns at the wheel with stops for meals and to walk Sam. Once in L.A. they spent a couple days at Patrice's place and then decided if T.K. wanted to meet her parents, then there was no time like the present. They left Sam with T.K.'s parents and hit the road. Christmas in Albuquerque, because of its huge Hispanic population, is celebrated with relish. Everywhere luminarias—flaming candles set in paper sacks with their bottoms filled with sand for stability—line streets, staircases of homes and businesses and doorways.

Patrice loved the way they looked all around the city. She and T.K. had helped place the illuminated bags along the walk leading to the Sutton ranch house, a sprawling one-story structure. The house, architecturally Spanish in style, sat in the middle of a thousand acres that had been owned by the Suttons for generations.

Today, December 24, was the second day since their arrival, and she thought T.K. was enjoying his visit so far. Right now, he was out herding the cattle to the south pasture with her father; her brothers, Luke and Patrick; and a couple of ranch hands.

Patrice was standing at the big picture window in the kitchen, peering outside hoping to see T.K. riding up soon with the rest of the men to stable their horses and come inside for Christmas Eve dinner, which she and her mother; her sister, Keira; and her sister-in-law, Nina, had been preparing all day.

Cady Sutton came to stand beside her. "Worried about him?" she asked, showing dimples in both cheeks. She, like the rest of the women, was dressed casually in slacks, a shirt and comfortable shoes. Traditionally they dressed for Christmas dinner but not for the meal the night before. After the meal, they would pile into cars and go to their church for the Christmas Eve service. The dress there was also casual because a lot of the families who attended were of modest means, and the clergy preferred a good turnout rather than a fashionable congregation.

At their church, the Christmas Eve service was all about the children. The congregation's children put on a play, and mothers and fathers inevitably tried to capture it on film. It was Patrice's favorite part of the holidays.

She remembered portraying Mary when she was seven. She considered it her first starring role.

"No, I'm not worried about him," she answered softly. "He's a good rider. I just hope they don't try to test him or something."

"You know your father," said her mother with a short laugh.

Yes, Patrice knew her father. He was a shameless practical joker, and he was probably pulling a prank on her unsuspecting sweetie right now. Her brothers would be happy to join in the fun.

T.K. could have sworn that Mr. Sutton was taking them in circles, and they had passed this way before. But he rode beside Patrice's father without protesting. They were supposed to meet up with the other four men and head back to the ranch. He and Mr. Sutton had herded the cattle from the south end while the other four men had taken the north end, and now the cattle was grazing on the sparse grass that grew in the south field. He had been amazed at the size of the herd, more than seven hundred head. He'd never seen that many cows in one place before.

He supposed it was obvious to these Southwestern men that he was a city boy. He didn't let that bother him, though. Like most new skills, he was excited about learning how to herd cattle the right way.

Suddenly Patrick Sutton pulled on his horse's reins

and stopped the animal. He listened intently. "What's that?" He nervously peered behind them.

It was dusk, and although T.K. had twenty-twenty vision, it was difficult to clearly see anything in the distance because of snow flurries.

Then he heard something moving in the brush not twenty feet away from them. His mount whinnied and took a few steps backward as if it were afraid of whatever was in the brush. "Be perfectly still," Patrick Sutton warned him. "I believe we've got a mountain lion on our trail."

Instead of being afraid, T.K. was thrilled. He got to see a mountain lion in its natural habitat! He wished he had brought his digital camera with him. Wait, he had his phone on him, and it had a built-in camera. He was reaching inside his coat to retrieve his cell phone from his shirt pocket when Luke leaped from the cover of the brush with a growl that could have been that of a mountain lion.

"What the hell!" T.K. cried and almost fell off his horse.

Mr. Sutton laughed so hard *he* nearly fell off *his* horse. For a moment, T.K. looked from father to son, confused. Then he burst out laughing, too.

"What were you digging in your pocket for?" Mr. Sutton asked. "Were you going to call the police?"

"No," T.K. admitted, "I thought I could get a photo of the mountain lion."

Patrick Sutton really laughed then. "Son, that may not

be the brightest idea." He nudged his horse closer so he could fondly pound T.K. on the back. "You're okay!"

Laughing, Luke, Patrick and the ranch hands, Jim and Charlie, came out of hiding then, and they rode companionably back to the ranch. T.K. had enjoyed his time with them.

Once they were back at the ranch, they took their horses to the stable, removed their saddles, rubbed the horses down, gave them fresh grain and water and then went into the ranch house through the kitchen door.

The women welcomed the six men back, wives going to their husbands to help them out of their coats and hanging them up. Patrice helped T.K. out of his coat. She watched him closely, trying to discern if his afternoon with the men had been a positive experience for him. He was looking at her just as intently, with longing. She could feel the sexual tension between them, like the air was charged with electricity. They had not made love since they'd been here. She didn't feel comfortable being intimate in her parents' house. He respected her wishes. But right now, he looked like he could kiss her until she passed out. Her temperature rose just thinking about it.

"Are you okay?" she asked softly.

T.K. bent and inhaled her scent. It turned him on more than he already had been. "God, I miss holding you," he whispered.

Patrice blushed and said, "Yeah, I know how you feel." She hung the coat on the rack near the door and walked back to him. "What happened out there?" she asked, concerned.

"I don't know what you mean," T.K. said. "We moved the cattle to the south pasture."

"I know you moved the cattle to the south pasture," whispered Patrice urgently. "I mean, what did my dad and my brothers do to you? I know them. They did something to test your mettle, as my daddy puts it."

T.K. laughed shortly. "Darlin', they were on their best behavior." He wasn't going to tell her about the mountain lion prank. He was in the men's club now, and the best way to get out of it was by shooting off at the mouth about activities done in private. He would take his cue from her father and brothers. If they remained silent, so would he.

Soon they sat down to eat. Keira's husband, Dr. Jorge Lopez, who was a general practitioner at a local hospital, had arrived and was sitting next to his wife at the table. Cady had seated all of the couples side by side except for herself and Patrick. He was at one end of the table, a ranch hand sitting near him and she was at the other end with a ranch hand next to her.

Everyone bowed their heads as Patrick Sr. said the prayer. "Father, we come to you on the eve of what many believe is your son's day of birth. Now, it may be and it may not be, but you have to admit, Lord, our hearts are in the right place. Thanks for your blessings year-round. We try to always remember that material possessions come and go, but love for your family remains constant, as it should. So thank you for increasing our fold, two babies on the way. That's the best news in a long time. Amen!"

"Amen," everyone said, and conversation commenced as dishes were passed from person to person until everyone had filled their plates.

Patrice heard pieces of conversation at the large table, Keira asking Jorge if he was still on call or could spend the rest of the evening with her. He unfortunately had to return to the hospital after dinner. "Someone's covering for me until I get back."

Patrice's heart had gone out to her sister when she saw the disappointment written on her pretty face. Being a doctor's wife wasn't easy.

Beside her Luke was asking T.K. how much of the stunt work he did in his movies. T.K. had laughed. "As few as I can. Generally, though, if you can see my face, it's me.

"If you can't, it's probably a stuntman."

Luke found this fascinating. "That was really you swinging from one building to another using a piece of the building's awning?"

"Yeah, but I was only about fifteen feet off the ground," T.K. told him. "There wasn't much danger involved."

"It looked like you were much higher than that," Luke said, sounding disappointed.

"That's the magic of movies," T.K. said. "They make you believe you're seeing what they want you to see."

T.K. began asking him questions. "Patty tells me you're in college. What're you majoring in?"

"Business administration," Luke told him. "I'll use what I learn to run the ranch more efficiently." Luke looked sheepishly at his father who was sitting at the end of the table. "Pops won't admit it, but he's old school and things could run smoother around here."

His father, who had sharp ears, couldn't let that slide. "This ranch has run efficiently for over a hundred years. There is nothing new under the sun about ranching. It's hard work. You can't calculate hard work on some computer. You have to get out there in the wind and the rain and the snow and do it!"

"Now, Patrick, that isn't what Luke means," Cady spoke up. Everyone's attention was now on the argument between father and son. "He just thinks that with some financial planning you could get more of a return for all that hard work you do. I don't see anything radical about his thinking. You hate doing the books anyway—always have. I end up doing them, and I'll be happy when someone takes over the job!"

Patrick stared down the table at his wife, sitting at the opposite end. "I didn't know that's how you felt."

"Well, now you do," said Cady, sitting up straighter on her chair and giving him a defiant look. "So stop getting on Luke's case every time he mentions running the ranch more efficiently."

"Yes, Mrs. Sutton," said Patrick Sr. obediently with a soft look in his eyes.

Patrice noticed everyone had gone back to their individual conversations now that the altercation between her parents had been amicably resolved. Or had it? Patrick Sr. got up out of his chair and strode to the end of the table, pulled Cady to her feet and hugged her. "You're a spirited filly. That's why I love you." Then he kissed her.

Laughter and applause erupted from those around the table.

And kissed her...

"That's right, Daddy Sutton, lay one on her!" Nina cried.

And kissed her...

"Um, Pops, your food's getting cold," Luke said nervously.

And kissed her...

"We'd just as well finish dinner," Patrice said. "This might take a while."

Finally, Patrick Sr. let his wife up for air. Cady was smiling and starry eyed. "You're a damn good kisser. That's why I married *you*." She sighed and walked back to her chair at the table. "What is everybody looking at? Yes, mature people still have a passion for one another. Now eat!"

T.K. laughed softly at Patrice's side. "I like your parents."

"Apparently they still like each *other* pretty well, too," Patrice said, smiling. She had been warmed by her parents' display of long-held passion. She reached for T.K.'s hand and he gave it to her. "I'm glad you came."

He smiled at her. "So am I." He felt inspired at that moment, inspired by the love in this room and inspired by the woman at his side.

Still holding her hand, he rose, bringing her to a standing position with him. He cleared his throat. "I have something to say," he announced.

He felt Patrice squeeze his hand. He pulled her close to his side, his arm wrapped around her, and he felt her relax against him. "I know my showing up with Patrice was a surprise. She didn't call ahead to say she was bringing me, and I know some of you have been wondering why she brought me." He looked at Nina specifically because he had overheard her speculating with Patrick about why Patrice had brought him home for Christmas. She'd said they were probably in love. "You were right, Nina," he told her now.

Nina grinned and danced excitedly on her chair. "I knew it!"

"You knew what, sweetie?" asked Cady.

Looking into Patrice's upturned face, T.K. said, "She knew that I'm in love with your daughter."

"Son, anybody looking at you looking at her coulda told you that," said Patrick Sr.

"I love him, too," Patrice said softly.

This brought awed silence from her family. They knew Patrice didn't take the love word lightly. This was a momentous occasion.

Cady's eyes filled with tears. She picked up her cloth napkin and dabbed at them. Looking at T.K., she said, "Go on, son."

Smiling, T.K.'s gaze went from Cady to Patrick Sr. "Mr. and Mrs. Sutton, I asked Patrice to bring me to meet you because I want to ask her to be my wife. This doesn't come as a surprise to Patty because we've already discussed it. What she doesn't know is that I'm going to ask her now, in front of her family." He reached inside his shirt pocket and produced a beautiful diamond solitaire ring set in platinum.

"When did you…?" Patrice began, wondering when he'd had time to go ring shopping.

Then she remembered that man in the black suit who had shown up at his parents' house with his lawyer. Patrice had thought they were in his dad's study discussing the situation with Aisha, who had been temporarily appeased by a shopping trip for new clothes to fit her postpregnancy body. She had promised to think about her next step until after the New Year. Then they would sit down and figure out what was best for Mira. "Your lawyer brought the jeweler with him," she said to T.K.

"Sharp mind," T.K. said. He got down on one knee and the other women in the room let out a collective sigh. "Patrice Catherine Sutton, would you do me the honor of becoming my wife?" He looked up at her with a hopeful, almost painful expression.

T.K. had to remember to breathe. What if she was too surprised by the gesture and wasn't ready to say yes?

"Yes!" Patrice shouted.

"I think they heard that in Santa Fe," Patrice's dad joked amid good-natured laughter.

T.K. rose and put the ring on Patrice's finger. It fit perfectly—another surprise. How had he known her ring size? She had noticed the gentleman in the black suit observing her a bit closely. At the time, she had thought he was kind of creepy. Now she supposed he was simply good at guessing a woman's ring size.

Patrice kissed her fiancé. She never imagined she could be this happy. Everyone got up and congratulated them with hugs and kisses. Cady hugged her daughter so tightly that Patrice feared for her ribs. Looking into her eyes, Cady said, "This is the one who owns your heart, then?"

"Yes, Momma," Patrice said, tears in her eyes.

"I'm happy for you," said Cady. "He's a good boy. Real strapping, too. You'll have strong children." She eyed Patrice. "You're not…?"

Patrice laughed shortly. "No, Momma."

Cady smiled. "I was hoping for three, but I shouldn't be greedy." She threw her arms around her daughter's neck and hugged her again. "You can work on it on the honeymoon."

Patrice continued to laugh as she received hugs from everyone else.

Finally, after things had settled down, the meal was

eaten and a sense of calm descended on the diners. There was plenty to be grateful for that day.

Outside, snow fell, and the luminarias, although in some of the paper bags the candles had gone out, continued to illuminate the cold night.

Chapter 12

On Christmas morning, everyone gathered around the kitchen table for breakfast. Patrick and Nina had stayed over, as had Keira, who saw no point in going home since her husband wouldn't be there. Patrice had gotten up early to help her mother prepare a big breakfast of homemade biscuits, scrambled eggs, sausages, fresh fruit and coffee.

T.K. strode into the room looking well-rested and handsome in his Western wear. He smiled at those assembled there. He was the last to arrive. The ranch hands, Jim and Charlie, who both appeared to him to be Native American, were at the table. He supposed they didn't have family in the area with which to spend Christmas. The Suttons treated them like family.

"Good morning," he said heartily. Everyone returned his greeting.

Patrice kissed him on the cheek. "Good morning," she said softly. "Sleep well?"

"Not without you," he whispered and took great delight in seeing her blush.

After everyone was seated, Cady said the blessing. "Dear Lord, thank you for another beautiful day, and yesterday wasn't bad, either. Amen."

"She's more succinct than your dad," said T.K. to Patrice.

Patrice smiled. She was glad he liked her parents. "She's a woman of few words but plenty of action, like her eldest daughter."

She blushed again when she realized what she had sounded like. Or perhaps her mind was hearing sexual innuendos where there were none because she wanted T.K. so badly. Now that she had made love to him, she knew exactly what he felt like, and she missed that closeness. After three days without him, the deprivation was beginning to affect her.

T.K. didn't appear to associate the word *action* with anything sexual, though. She smiled at him again and began eating. His gaze went to her naked ring finger. "Where's your ring?"

"In my room," she said. "You don't think I'm going to wear it while kneading biscuit dough?"

"I bought it for you to wear during everyday activities,"

T.K. said casually. "It's just a ring, babe. If it breaks I'll get you another one."

Patrice gave him a steely-eyed glare. "It's not just a ring. It's the one you picked out for me, and I'm going to take care of it. Tell your alter ego that I want Trevor back."

They were trying to keep their voices down, but it was apparent to the others at the table that an argument was brewing.

"Have you two thought about a wedding date yet?" Nina interrupted them, hoping to dispel the bad vibes. "I've always thought spring was the perfect time for a wedding."

"Oh, yes, it'll be beautiful here in Albuquerque in the spring," Cady said. "You *are* going to have it in our church, aren't you?"

T.K. was grateful for the interruption. He didn't know why Patrice had gotten testy with him when he had mentioned buying another ring if something happened to the five-carat solitaire. He thought he was being magnanimous. He knew she had admitted she was frugal, but he was one of the richest men in the country. What did the cost of an engagement ring matter to him?

Patrice ignored the overtures to ease the tension between her and T.K. She had to make him understand once and for all that material possessions weren't to be tossed about like confetti. Yeah, he was stinking rich, but that didn't mean he could be so nonchalant about a ring that he'd given her out of love. If something like that was interchangeable to him, what about her? Was she interchangeable as well?

"May I see you in private?" she asked as she rose.

T.K. immediately got up. "Lead the way."

When they left the kitchen, Nina turned to Patrick, distressed. "Why did he have to say that about the ring? Women are sentimental about their engagement rings. You can't just chalk it up as a loss and buy another one if something happens to it. It's special."

Patrick glanced at the one-carat diamond on his wife's finger. It had been all he could afford. He took her hand in his. He had almost been ashamed to present her with it when he had proposed. "You like your ring?" he asked softly.

Nina kissed his face enthusiastically. "I love it!" she said.

Patrick smiled at her. He adored her.

In her bedroom, Patrice closed the door after she and T.K. were inside. Turning to face him, she said, "You may think I'm being unreasonable because I got angry when you suggested replacing my ring if I should lose it or damage it, but this is important to me, Trevor. Money can't fix everything. What was touching and special last night when you proposed you made commonplace and trivial when you suggested I treat the ring like an everyday bauble. Come on, that's my engagement ring. You chose it. It'll always be special to me."

"Honestly, I was only joking," T.K. tried to explain.

Patrice eyed him skeptically. "And maybe showing off a little in front of the soon-to-be-in-laws?"

T.K. thought about it and laughed suddenly. Maybe he had been bragging a bit. It was hard being T. K. McKenna without being perhaps a touch arrogant. "So what if I want your family to know that I can take care of you?"

"Believe me, baby, they're not impressed with a big Hollywood hotshot. They're more impressed with the guy who would go with them to move the cows to the south pasture. They don't want their daughter and sister to marry some guy with plenty of money who isn't going to cherish her. They think of Hollywood people with horror when they hear of all the divorces and infidelity out there."

"Divorces and infidelity happen everywhere," T.K. reminded her.

"Yes, but Hollywood has theirs broadcast all over the media," Patrice said with a tired sigh.

T.K. looked deeply into her eyes and heaved a sigh. "I looked like a fool."

"No, you didn't. You were just being an alpha male who takes care of his woman. Every male in that kitchen is an alpha male. They understand you." She walked into his open arms. "But we women have to tame you, sometimes gentle you down a bit."

"Make us putty in your hands," said T.K. as his mouth descended on hers.

It had been a while since they'd kissed like this. They were both hungry for it, and because of that, the kiss aroused them that much more. Patrice melted into his embrace, her body molded to his. She could not get close enough. Their tongues took pleasure from being reunited. It was so sweet that they stood there and kissed for several minutes and didn't at first hear the knocking on the door.

Patrice hadn't locked the door. She'd just shut it. She rarely locked doors in her parents' house. "Coming in," called Cady.

They flew apart, guilty expressions on their faces. Patrice was glad she hadn't put on lipstick this morning because if she had it would be smeared all over T.K.'s mouth.

"Are you two all right?" Cady asked. "We were worried about you. Don't want you calling off the wedding before we've even planned it."

Patrice and T.K. stood there with their arms around each other's waists, presenting a lovely picture of togetherness. "We're over it," Patrice said of their argument. "No worries."

"Okay, I'll leave you alone, then," said Cady, smiling. "Breakfast's getting cold."

When she'd gone, they looked at one another and laughed. "Good thing she showed up," T.K. joked. "We would have been naked in a couple minutes."

Patrice knew he was right. Her body was still tingling with pleasure.

T.K. bent his head to kiss her again, and she ducked underneath his arm and headed for the door. "No, no, let's eat breakfast and make up some excuse about seeing the city. Then we can get a hotel room." Her gaze was serious. "I won't be able to cope if I don't make love to you soon."

T.K. liked the sound of that. He followed her back to the kitchen.

"Did she take you to the woodshed?" asked Patrick Sr. as soon as they sat down.

T.K. nodded and smiled at Patrice. "She really let me have it," he said.

Patrice kicked him underneath the table.

Later, when Patrice was helping her mother with the dishes, Cady, who was washing while Patrice dried, cleared her throat. "My, oh, my, the way that man looks at you reminds me of the way your daddy used to look at me when we first met, like I was something good to eat and he was starving to death!"

Patrice looked at her mother with a shocked expression, but her eyes were lit with humor. "Momma, you know we kids don't like to think of you and Daddy having a sex life. We were immaculate conceptions—all of us."

Cady laughed. "You're a fine actress, darling, but not that good. You take delight in the fact that your father and I still love each other. That gives you and T.K. hope. It tells you that marriages can last even in the twenty-first century. As for passion, I say grab all of it while you can. There's a reason God made us passionate. It was to keep the family going. Family is important. Sometimes, it's the only thing that's important. Jobs come and go. There are fair-weather friends. But when a man and a woman come together in marriage and have children together, if they really love each other, now that's worth getting up for every morning."

Patrice had finished drying the dishes, and she now began putting them away in the cabinets above the sink. She regarded her mother. "Was there any time you thought you had made a mistake by marrying Daddy?" she asked. "I know you come from a well-to-do family in Charleston. I remember our girl cousins being so prim and proper and how much they looked down their noses at us. I never told you, but I was not happy going down South. They never made me feel welcome. I wondered where all that Southern hospitality they talked about was."

Her mother laughed shortly. "I never fit in, either. My parents were both born into well-to-do families in Charleston. Theirs was a match made to unite two rich families. I don't believe they were ever happy together. It's sad, really. When I was growing up, I always told myself that I would not marry for anything except love—not only love but a *passionate* love. Your grandparents, God rest their souls, never expressed passion for anything. It was such a white-bread world. When I came to Albuquerque with some friends from college, I experienced something magical. Here was a land of spices. People here were of different nationalities behaving as if they didn't care about their differences. What they cared about was a sense of community and their families. Then when I met your father, who was trying to make a go of the ranch on his own, I saw a man of strength and character. He wasn't bad-looking either. We fell in love almost instantly. I mean this sincerely, my love. The first time we looked at each other, we knew that there was something powerful between us. I tried to fight it because I was this little Southern girl who'd been brought up by strict parents. I'd never gone out on a date until I was eighteen. At twenty-one, though, and fresh out of college, I exulted in my independence. I told my friends they would have to go back to Charleston without me. I was staying and marrying your father."

"That didn't sit well with your parents, I imagine," Patrice said.

Her mother chuckled. "They actually came after me, but by the time they got here, your father and I had gotten married at the courthouse and had consummated the marriage several times to my utter satisfaction. I've never regretted marrying your father and staying in New Mexico."

Patrice guffawed. "All right, now!"

"Three months after we were married I found out I was pregnant with you," Cady said wistfully.

"You two worked fast," Patrice said, still laughing.

"That's why I made the honeymoon comment last night after you got engaged. We are very fertile women.

It doesn't take too many tries to make a baby in this family."

That was food for thought for Patrice. Maybe condoms weren't a good enough form of birth control for her and T.K. Work-wise she was booked well into the next year. She shouldn't get pregnant for the next two years. However, if all precautions were a total bust and she turned up pregnant anyway, there was no doubt she would have the baby.

"I'll keep that in mind," Patrice said of the women in her family being very fertile.

Cady gave her a smile and a quick hug. "So, what are you and T.K. doing on your last day in town?"

"I thought I'd take him to a few of my favorite places, if you can spare me in the kitchen for a few hours," Patrice told her.

"I'll put Keira and Nina to work," her mother said. "They've been allowing you to help me in the kitchen since they know you love to cook. You and T.K. have fun."

Half an hour later, Patrice and T.K. were in his SUV with her at the wheel. T.K. sat in the passenger seat with his sunglasses on, smiling. "Where're we going?"

"We're going to Old Town," Patrice said as she drove. It was an overcast day, looked like snow again in the afternoon. She breathed a sigh of relief. It wasn't as cold here as it had been in Wyoming.

"Are we going sightseeing today?" T.K. asked, watching her profile. He knew where they would eventually end up, but perhaps Patrice wanted to go someplace else so that when they returned to the ranch she could say they'd been seeing the town and not have to totally lie about that whereabouts.

"No, we're going to Hotel Albuquerque at Old Town," Patrice told him. "It's in the middle of the historic Old Town Plaza and museum district, an area that's been there over 400 years."

"You seem a little nervous," T.K. observed.

"I wish we had left a bag in the car when we arrived, but we didn't. I had a hard time sneaking an overnight bag and a garment bag into the car. There's always somebody around the house."

T.K. laughed. "Why would you sneak a bag out of the house? We aren't going to spend the night."

"You don't check into a luxury hotel without bags," Patrice said, perfectly serious. "They don't rent rooms by the hour."

T.K. laughed harder. "Darlin', you are so innocent in some ways. As long as you've got the money to pay for the room they don't care if you use it for an hour or a month.

"That's your business."

"Okay," Patrice said skeptically. "I'm not walking into that hotel empty-handed, that's all."

"You're so stubborn," said T.K.

"Yes, I am," agreed Patrice.

The minute she and T.K. began walking toward the registration desk, however, Patrice was glad she was taking steps to be careful. Behind the desk was Lucy Lopez. She'd had no idea Lucy worked there! Lucy hadn't looked up and seen her yet.

Patrice turned to T.K. "You're going to have to get the room on your own. The woman behind the desk is Keira's sister-in-law. Keep your sunglasses on. Hopefully she won't recognize you. I'll wait for you by the elevators." She handed him the bags.

T.K. humored her. It was obvious she was concerned that it would get back to her family that they'd gone to a hotel while they were visiting.

At the desk, he registered as Trevor Kennedy Mc-Kenna. Lucy Lopez smiled at him, her eyes roving over his muscular frame and his face, but she didn't seem to connect him with the actor, T. K. McKenna.

Room key in hand, he joined Patrice at the bank of elevators. Several other people were waiting for the conveyance as well. He leaned down to whisper in her ear, "Mission accomplished. I don't think she recognized me."

"Good," Patrice whispered back.

On the ride up to their floor, they stood in the back of the elevator, arms around each other's waists. The other five passengers were obviously tourists. They were talking about historic Old Town and their visit to see the annual River of Lights display at the Rio Grande Botanic Garden.

"We went there, didn't we?" asked T.K.

Patrice nodded. "Yes, the first day we were here,

all the Christmas lights?" she said, giving him a brief description of the attraction in order to enhance his memory.

"Oh, yeah, they were something else," he said appreciatively.

One of the women, an attractive black woman in her mid-thirties, turned to look at T.K. and cautiously asked, "Aren't you T. K. McKenna?"

T.K. laughed shortly. He pulled off his sunglasses and said to Patrice, "I told you I looked like T. K. McKenna with my head shaved." Then he said back at the woman, "*She* even thinks so."

Patrice smiled at the woman. "Please don't encourage him. I'll never hear the end of it. No, my fiancé isn't T. K. McKenna."

The woman squinted up at T.K. and wrinkled her nose. "Come to think of it, he's not as tall as you are, is he? They always look bigger on the screen. I hear Tom Cruise is only five-seven. He looks bigger in the movies." She smiled at T.K. again. "But I'm with you. You do look an awful lot like him."

When they got to their suite, Patrice unlocked the door and stumbled into it laughing. "We go to all that trouble of getting around Lucy unnoticed and then you get recognized on the elevator!"

T.K. frowned. "I hated confusing the poor woman. But I did it to save your reputation." He laughed shortly. "You should have seen your face when you spotted Keira's sister-in-law behind the registration desk. You were bug-eyed."

Patrice put her shoulder bag on the foyer table and went to him to relieve him of the bags he was carrying. She placed them beside her bag on the table. With this done, she got out of her coat and hung it on the hall tree next to the door and turned to face him. T.K. had already removed his coat and thrown it onto a nearby chair. His gaze roamed over her luscious body in jeans and a royal blue sweater. Patrice took a deep breath as she watched him, her chest rising and falling.

No words were needed at this point. They fell on each other, kissing hungrily. T.K. pulled her sweater over her head and kissed her again. Her chest pressed against his, but she wasn't satisfied with the feel of his shirt. She broke off the kiss long enough to unbutton his denim shirt and pull it off him. He undid the clasps on her bra, and finally, they were skin to skin. They both sighed contentedly. Her nipples hardened at the first touch of his skin on hers. T.K. jerked her roughly against him, then picked her up fireman style and tossed her butt-first onto the king-size bed. He took the time to remove her shoes and drop them onto the floor. Patrice unbuttoned her button-fly jeans, and he grasped them by the hems and pulled them off her. All that was left on her were a very small pair of panties.

T.K. got out of his athletic shoes, socks and jeans. He wore boxer-briefs. They were molded to his body, and the bulge in them was quite impressive. Patrice looked at that bulge and suddenly remembered. No condoms. She didn't have a single condom with her. "Condoms?" she croaked, looking desperately at T.K., willing him to say he'd remembered them.

He chuckled and went to get his wallet out of his jeans' pocket. "The old standbys," he said as he held up a couple for her to see.

"Not too old, I hope," said Patrice.

"Trust me," he said as he knelt on the bed, tossed the condoms in their wrappers onto the bed where they'd be within easy reach and grasped the waistband of her panties and began pulling. Patrice lifted her hips a bit to help him. When the panties had been tossed behind him, he spread her legs and simply looked at her a moment. He loved everything about her body, how her full breasts felt in the palms of his hands, how her firm round bottom looked like a perfectly formed peach. He leaned down and kissed her mouth. She wrapped her arms and her legs around his body. She sighed with pleasure, and her tongue made love to his. She might have all the physical attributes of every other woman he had made love to in the past, but she certainly used them in a unique, thoroughly satisfying fashion. With her, he knew that she was enjoying herself as much as he was. She pushed it to the limit every time. Because of that, it felt new and exciting every time they made love.

She gestured for him to roll her over so that she would be on top. He happily obliged.

He knew what she was after, getting him out of his

boxer-briefs. He admitted that he liked it when she released him and held him in her hands. He moaned softly when she reenacted the scene that had been in his mind.

Patrice held him in her hand. His hard member pulsed with a life of its own. She bent and licked the tip. He throbbed in her hand. She took this as an indication it was time to put the condom on. He never liked coming before her; he said it made no sense since he would have to wait a few minutes before he was hard again. He wanted her to get her pleasure first.

So she took her pleasure. After putting the condom on him, she climbed onto his member and rode him until he was crying out for release. She had come once and was approaching another explosion.

Their bodies had a thin layer of perspiration, and it was with sweet pain coupled with intense pleasure, a few minutes later, that she cried out as another climax rocked her and he grabbed her hips and pumped her hard before crying out in release himself. She fell onto his chest a bit breathlessly and kissed his mouth, biting his lower lip, felt his member throb some more inside of her and then suckled his lower lip.

Momentarily, she laid her head on his chest. T.K. sighed. He even liked it when she lay on top of him afterward, their bodies slick, warm and satisfied. "It's always over way too soon for me," he said softly in her ear.

She looked into his eyes. "Yes, but I like this time together, just holding you."

T.K. smiled. He didn't want to ever be parted from her for any reason. He thought about their first argument. He would try to be more sensitive about her workingwoman sensibilities and not be so blasé about the cost of things. Had he been a rich man for so long that he no longer knew how to think like the average American? Had he become elitist? He hated to think that he had. He would work on that.

Patrice had closed her eyes, and for a moment, he thought she was sleeping. Then she opened them and smiled at him. "How about a shower and we do that again?"

Chapter 13

"**D**rive carefully," Cady told them as Patrice and T.K. climbed into the SUV for the trip back to Los Angeles, this time with T.K. at the wheel. The household had assembled on the front stoop to see them off. When Patrice had kissed her father goodbye he'd said for her ears only, "He passed the mountain lion test. He's worth hanging on to."

Patrice had playfully punched him on the arm. "Daddy, no, you didn't!" It wasn't the first time her father had taken advantage of Luke's unique way with animal sounds and used that talent to pull a prank on somebody.

She wasn't going to let him get off scot-free this time, though. "Momma, did you hear about what Daddy and

Luke did to T.K. while they were out with the cattle the day before yesterday?"

Her father was trying to shush her, but she wouldn't let him. "They made him think he was being attacked by a mountain lion."

"What?" cried Cady, going to playfully grab her husband by the ear.

"Ouch, woman!" said Patrick. "We didn't hurt the boy. He was a good sport about it. Tell them, T.K.!"

"Really, Mrs. Sutton, I got a good laugh out of it. I was only disappointed I didn't get a photo of the mountain lion."

Cady laughed. "You were going to photograph a mountain lion?" She turned to Patrice. "Baby, tell him on the trip home how crazy that sounds. And I'll handle your father." That was when she'd told them to drive carefully, and she and T.K. had driven off with her looking back fondly at her family standing on the front stoop.

"What did she mean by that?" T.K. asked.

"Mountain lions attack people and livestock. They kill and maim. They're extremely dangerous. If you ever see one, don't stick around to take its photo. Just recently, a boy was dragged off by one. His father managed to fight it off, but the little boy was badly mangled. It took him months to recover."

"That's terrible," T.K. said, returning his attention to the road. "I'm really a greenhorn, aren't I? There I was reaching for my cell phone to take a photo. I should have known something was up when your dad led me in circles."

"But you trusted him not to lead you astray," Patrice said. "He didn't mean anything by it. He was just having fun, but Momma and I don't like it when he does it to unsuspecting people."

"Don't be too hard on him for my sake," T.K. told her. "I took it as an initiation into the Sutton men's club. Really, I laughed as hard as the rest of them."

"Okay, I'm letting it go," Patrice said. "I just wanted your visit to be a pleasant one."

"It was. Men don't think the same way women do. You're angry because you think they scared me just to get a laugh. But they didn't do it for a laugh. They did it to let me know that they accept me. That means a lot to me."

Patrice shook her head. She got him now. It was true that in her and her mother's opinion her father's prank-playing was incomprehensible. But perhaps that was simply one of the ways that men and women differed. Women generally didn't get *The Three Stooges,* either, but many men found them hilarious. "All right," she conceded. "I will defer to you when it comes to my father's sense of humor."

T.K. reached over and squeezed her hand. "He's a good guy, your dad."

Patrice couldn't argue with that.

The first order of business when they got back to Los Angeles was to go to his parents' house and collect Sam, but there was also the matter of telling his parents that he and Patrice had gotten engaged on Christmas Eve.

It was sundown when they got to the Beverly Hills mansion. The house had belonged to T.K., but he had given it to his parents and moved to Malibu after they had agreed to move out here. He had always thought the house was too big for him alone. Now he had his Malibu house that he loved, and the house in Beverly Hills was occupied by family whom he visited often and whose friends and relatives visited often. So it was nice for them to have plenty of room to accommodate their guests.

T.K. had a key to the house and also knew the security code, so he let himself and Patrice into the house. He stood in the foyer a moment, listening. Usually, there was music on somewhere in the house when he entered it. Both his parents were jazz fans and would have Grover Washington Jr. or some other jazz great's music piped in over the sound system.

The house was silent.

He and Patrice looked at each other. He could tell she also felt the uneasiness he was feeling. Where was everybody? Also, where was Sam, who usually was jumping up on him and licking his face by now?

He took Patrice by the hand and headed for the kitchen where he could usually find someone as it was the hub of the house.

"Hello!" he called. "Anybody at home?"

"If they were going off for the day, wouldn't they have

phoned you to tell you about it?" Patrice asked. "They were expecting you back today."

T.K. stopped in his tracks, let go of her hand and checked his cell phone. He had forgotten to turn it back on. He checked the messages. Sure enough, his mother had phoned him at least three times. He listened to the first message. "Trevor, Aisha is gone, and she's taken Mira with her. I went to check up on her when she didn't come down for breakfast. I thought maybe she'd had a rough night with Mira. Mira's been keeping her up nights. She didn't leave a message or anything. I'm worried about them. Your father and I don't agree on what to do. He says we should call the police, but I don't think they'll look for an adult right away—a child, yes, but she's twenty-six. Please call as soon as you can." T.K. checked the date of the message. It had been on Christmas Day. Aisha had been missing for more than twenty-four hours.

He looked at Patrice, who was watching him with a concerned expression. "Aisha took off with Mira. My parents don't know where she is. I've got two more messages to listen to."

He listened to number two. "Your dad and I are going out to look for her. We're taking Sam with us. He loved to be around Mira so much that we're hoping against hope that somehow he'll know where she is. I have one of her little sweaters that she's worn with me, and I'm letting him sniff it. I know he isn't a hound dog, but I'm desperate. Why would Aisha do this and make us worry?

She said she would talk to us after the holidays, and we would decide together what was best for her and Mira then. Is she so scared that we're going to try to take Mira from her that she ran? Trevor, please call."

T.K. was so angry at Aisha for putting his mother through such a stressful situation that he couldn't listen to the final message. He handed the phone to Patrice, and she listened. "It's the day after she left, and we're combing East Los Angeles. It's the only place we know of that she was known to have lived before she met Malcolm. I don't know why you haven't phoned yet, Trevor. I hope nothing's happened. I couldn't take it if something's happened to you, too."

Patrice handed him the phone. "They're looking for her in East L.A., with no luck so far. Call your mother, Trevor. She sounds upset."

T.K. took the phone and dialed his mother's cell phone number. Rose McKenna must have answered right away, because he started talking, "I'm sorry, I'm sorry. My phone was off. Where are you now? We'll come to you." His mother must have told him. He closed the cell phone and met Patrice's gaze. "They're on the way back home. They're exhausted. Damn it, I should have known that little user would do something like this as soon as I turned my back! I'm calling the cops."

Patrice was angry, too. It was wrong of Aisha to make everybody sick with worry. Mira was only a little over a month old; she was so vulnerable. What if Aisha did something stupid like leaving her with somebody untrustworthy? You heard horror stories about people abusing, even killing babies on the news all the time.

She had to remain calm for T.K.'s sake though. "What can you charge her with?" she asked reasonably. "She's Mira's only surviving parent. She has the right to take her anywhere she wants to. Hire a private detective to find her and then you can deal with her, but the police might be the wrong choice right now."

T.K. looked hurt that she didn't support his course of action. "You sound like you're on her side in the matter."

"I'm always on your side," Patrice assured him, "but think. She could be scared and confused, and she could come back home at any time. If she sees police cars all over the place, she's going to be reluctant to come to you for help."

"She shouldn't have taken Mira out of this house!" T.K. bellowed.

Patrice jumped. She'd never seen him in a rage before. He looked like he could tear someone apart with his bare hands. A thrill of fear shot through her. He was a big man. He probably *could* tear someone apart with his bare hands.

She took a step backward. "Calm down," she said softly. "Yes, she took Mira with her, but that doesn't mean she's run away for good. Maybe she needed to go someplace where she could think, be away from Malcolm's family for a while. I know you think you know everything you need to know about her, but maybe she's been grieving for Malcolm this whole time and she'll come to the realization that she does need help raising Mira, and she'll come back. Just think before you call the police. That's all I ask."

T.K.'s gaze was cold when he looked at her. To Patrice, it was like looking into the eyes of someone who was totally devoid of emotions—dead eyes.

"I really can't deal with your altruistic views right now, Patrice. I need to handle this and handle it swiftly." He was about to say more, but suddenly there was the sound of his mother's voice in the foyer shouting, "Trevor! We're home."

Sam ran into the room, smiling, tail wagging, totally happy to see them. Patrice was surprised when he came straight to her but then perhaps he'd sensed his master's frame of mind and thought he'd get a better reception from her.

She knelt and hugged him. He licked her face repeatedly. Patrice felt like crying. With another cold look in her direction, T.K. turned to go greet his parents. She heard them talking in the foyer, but from this distance their voices were not clear to her so she didn't know what they were saying.

T.K. returned to the kitchen alone. "I told them to go lie down and I'd bring dinner up to them," he explained tersely. "Alma, their housekeeper, went to visit family over the holidays."

Patrice rose and patted Sam on the head. "I can prepare something for them."

"No, you go home, I know you're probably tired," T.K. said with that dead look still in his eyes.

Patrice was hurt. Shouldn't she be here to support him? Why was he pushing her away? "I'm not tired," she told him with a tentative smile. "I'm concerned about Mira, too. I want to stay and help."

He didn't smile back. "Don't you get it?" he asked, his tone rough. "I have to act, and I don't want you around to pass judgment on me for my actions. Go home, Patrice."

"I never judged you," said Patrice. Tears sat in her eyes.

T.K. hated himself for putting those tears in her eyes. But she didn't live in the real world if she thought he could sit around and wait for some detective who didn't have the resources the police had to find Aisha and, more importantly, Mira. The longer he waited the farther she could go with his brother's child. It was critical that they do something now. Patrice was in the way with her idealistic view of life.

"Here," he said, walking toward her with his car keys in his outstretched hand. "Take my car and go home. I'll call you later."

Patrice took his keys and turned her back to him. She felt weak all of a sudden. He was treating her like this because she had disagreed with him about how he should deal with Aisha. She wouldn't argue with him further. Undoubtedly he was terrified right now, wondering if he'd ever see his niece again. She understood that. But how did he know what was in Aisha's mind and heart? He had seen the girl as only a gold digger from the beginning. He'd never given her a chance. Patrice had met her only twice, but both times the girl had struck her as scared and uncertain about her future. She was like any young woman who had grown up in poverty and latched onto a good thing only to have that good thing snatched away. She was adrift. Of course she was intimidated by T.K. and his family. She hoped that she and Mira would be okay wherever they were, and she regretted that comment she'd made when T.K. had told her Aisha had insisted he marry her. She'd told him to be wary of women like Aisha when she hadn't met her and had no idea what kind of woman she was. She only knew what T.K. had told her about her.

She turned back around to face him. "I'm really sorry this happened, Trevor. Call me if you need me." She left.

T.K. was stunned that she'd gone, even though he was the one who had asked her to leave. He felt out of control and unreasonable right now. He wanted to hit somebody. He wanted to throttle Aisha. He should never have invited her to stay. Then he would not have seen Mira and grown to love her in such a short time. It would have been better to have never known of her existence than to be experiencing this fear and pain.

He uttered an expletive and got his phone out of his pocket. He dialed Saul Abraham's number, and when he answered, he told him what had happened.

"If we can prove that she's incompetent, we have a chance of gaining custody," his lawyer told him after a few minutes of consulting with him. "If she tried to sell the child, for example, that would give you the chance to swoop in and take her away from her. But right now, you have no right to call in the police."

T.K. felt a pang of regret. His mother had said that maybe Aisha had run away because she was afraid they might try to take Mira away from her. Was that the impression he'd given her? No, he was certain he had assured her that he would support both her and Mira, not take Mira away. His conscience was clear.

Now that she'd behaved in this manner, she would have to be tracked down and dealt with, and perhaps Mira would have to be taken away from her mother for safety's sake.

But he hadn't initiated all this; Aisha had.

To be honest, Aisha had given him the impression that she didn't want to be a mother. She'd tried to force him to marry her so she could live in the lap of luxury. Then when he'd refused, she'd griped about being out of shape, and no man would want her and certainly wouldn't want her once they found out she had a kid. That hadn't sounded like a devoted mother to him. "All right," he told Saul Abraham. "Get a good detective on her trail as soon as possible."

He hung up, and that's when he remembered that Patrice had told him the same thing as his lawyer had just told him.

He looked around and realized he was alone in the kitchen. Where was Sam?

Patrice wiped at tears as she drove T.K.'s SUV across town to her bungalow. Sam sat in the passenger seat with his head out the window. He had followed her to the car and climbed in and had refused to budge. To be honest, she welcomed his company. "This is so wrong," she said to him. "I'll have to phone him when I get home and tell him you came home with me. I'll take you back in the morning. But for now, I don't think I want to see him."

Some part of her knew she should be making allowances for T.K.'s behavior. He was under a great deal of stress. However, some other part told her that no matter what kind of stress you might be under you didn't ostracize the people you loved.

She stopped at a market near her house to get Sam enough food to last a couple days. Then she drove on to the house. At the house, she let Sam into the fenced-in backyard so she wouldn't have to watch him while she got her luggage out of T.K.'s car.

After giving him something to eat and filling a bowl with fresh water for him, she left Sam in the kitchen while she went to the bathroom to shower. She hadn't been tired before her confrontation with T.K., but now she felt drained. After her shower, she went out to her bedroom and changed into pajamas and a robe. Sam came into the room, whining pitifully. Patrice should have known he would need to go out once more before they retired for the night. She glanced at the clock on the nightstand. It was only 7:45 p.m. It was not exactly the time she usually turned in for the night, but she couldn't think of anything more enticing right now than her bed. She wanted to sleep away this dreadful day and wake up tomorrow to find it had all been a bad dream.

She walked into the adjacent closet and changed into jeans, a long-sleeved shirt and leather slippers. Going back out to the room, she snapped her fingers at Sam. "Come on, boy, and don't give me any problems. I don't have your leash, and I don't feel like running all over the neighborhood looking for you. That's all I need, to lose his dog."

Oh, God, she'd forgotten to phone T.K. about Sam. She went to the get her cell phone from her purse on the bureau in her bedroom. She quickly dialed T.K.'s number. He didn't answer. After the beep, she said, "Don't worry about Sam, he's with me." That was all she said. It was all she felt like saying to him. As soon as she hung up, she felt guilty for being hurt. Was it childish on her part? Should she be self-sacrificing enough to forgive him his tone of voice, and that dead expression with which he'd regarded her? The man was hurting.

The man was hardheaded, intractable and arrogant. She loved him, but she didn't have to be in his presence while he was channeling Satan. She went to take Sam for a walk.

Her neighbor, Kay Schuster, an elderly woman who walked her schnauzer, Rolf, every evening about this time, called to her as soon as she and Sam hit the sidewalk. There was a park at the end of the street, and that's where they were headed. "Hi, Patrice. Did you adopt recently?" Sam let her rub his head. Rolf barked once with no enthusiasm, just to let Sam know that Kay was his human and not to get too familiar.

"No, he belongs to a friend. I'm just keeping him overnight," Patrice told her.

Kay, short and stout, with warm brown skin and long wavy gray hair that she wore in a ponytail most of the time, grinned at Sam. "Oh, he's handsome. What's his name?"

"Sam," Patrice said.

"He looks like a Sam," Kay said. They walked on. The evening air was cool but not cold. Neither needed a jacket, but a sweater would be welcome. "How was your Christmas?"

"Great," said Patrice. "I went to Albuquerque." She didn't feel she knew Kay well enough to tell her that not only did she go home for Christmas but she took her boyfriend home to meet her parents and had gotten engaged on Christmas Eve. They were hello-how're-you-doing neighbors, not intimate friends.

"Ah, yes," said Kay, "that's where you're from. I hear the city's really beautiful during the holidays."

"It is. It's magical," said Patrice. She told Kay about the luminarias.

They arrived at the park and the dogs ran off, circling one another tentatively at first, then engaging each other in a friendlier manner as the game progressed. "Do you think they ever worry about anything?" Patrice wondered aloud.

"Sure, they do," Kay said. "When they'll get their next meal, whether or not their mistress will be kind or cruel to them, things any living being worries about."

The two dogs were expressing so much joy that Patrice found it hard to believe they worried about anything.

Later, she made Sam a bed on the floor out of an old comforter she didn't use anymore. She left it in the living room, but when she turned her back on him, he took it between his teeth and dragged it after her. She wound up putting the makeshift bed in a corner of her bedroom, and he settled down atop it. He didn't go to sleep though; he simply watched her. She lay on her bed; he lay on his and they looked into each other's eyes. "What are you looking at?" Patrice asked. "Do you think I was unreasonable with your master?" Sam's expression didn't change. "He's the one who threw me out."

She needed to talk to someone besides Sam—Belana or Elle instead. Sitting up in bed, she tried Belana's number first. It went to voice mail. Because she didn't want to announce she was engaged over the phone, and at this point wasn't feeling too confident about her engagement anyway, she didn't leave a message. She dialed Elle's number.

Elle answered with an enthusiastic, "Patty, how are you, girl?"

Patrice burst into tears. "Awful," she said, sniffling.

Between sobs, she told Elle all about it. "I'm just praying that Aisha shows up. He looked like he was ready to kill somebody. He was so angry."

"He didn't threaten you?" Elle asked, concerned.

"Oh, no," Patrice was quick to deny. "I've never seen him so angry before. It scared me. But the anger wasn't directed at me. It was all for Aisha. I know he thinks she did this to spite him, as some sort of payback because he rebuffed her advances."

"She sounds really sad to me," said Elle. "I mean, her hold on Malcolm was tenuous at best because of his mental state. He probably couldn't have married her without his family's support, and they don't seem to like her. Then he died, and she was left alone to raise their baby. I would be going nuts, too."

"That was my point," Patrice told her friend. "But T.K. only thinks she's trying to manipulate him. Yes, she was a user, but from her point of view it was out of necessity."

"On the other hand," Elle said, "some users never learn their lessons and continue to use people even when they've been given the benefit of the doubt. T.K. is highly upset because she used his brother. He's not going to let her do the same thing to him."

"Oh, believe me," said Patrice, "that'll never happen. At the first sight of her, he's going to try to have her thrown in jail."

"If she does anything to jeopardize that child's safety, that's where she belongs," said Elle.

Patrice heard a baby's cry in the background. "How is Ariana?"

Elle laughed softly. "She's doing beautifully. She's crawling all over the place and pulling up. She'll probably take her first steps any day now. She's with her papa right now."

"As I recall, he dotes on her," Patrice said fondly.

"Sweetie, it's as if he's discovering love all over again. Seeing him with Ariana makes me miss the daddy I never had."

"He missed out on *you*," Patrice told her. "Anyway, you've got a stepfather who loves you. That makes up for it a bit, doesn't it?"

"It does. John is a wonderful man, and he adores Ariana, so that's good enough for me. She deserves to be cherished."

"Yes, she does," agreed Patrice.

"But back to you and T.K.," Elle said. "Don't let this cause a rift in your relationship."

Patrice sighed. "What can I do? He asked me to leave. I've never been so hurt."

"Lick your wounds and try again. You love him. I don't believe you've ever loved any other man in the way you describe how it is between you and T.K. You have to give it your best shot."

Patrice paused a long time before saying, "I will. Thanks for listening. I'd better go. Sam is still looking at me as if *I'm* the one with issues. Why'd I bring this nutty dog home with me?"

"Because you didn't want to be alone," said Elle, wise and wonderful as usual.

"Bye, sweetie, love you," said Patrice.

"I love you, too," Elle said with a note of a smile in her tone.

After Patrice hung up the phone, she lay down in bed and closed her eyes. Sam was still watching her. "Go to sleep, Sam."

She was drifting off to dreamland when her cell phone rang. She picked it up and checked the display. It was T.K. She let it go to voice mail.

Chapter 14

The next day Patrice was prepared to drop Sam off, give T.K. back his car keys and leave. She would phone for a cab as she walked down the street on her way back home. She was still upset with T.K.

However, when she arrived at the house, she was met by Rose McKenna, who grasped her by the arm and pulled her into the house. Sam ran inside and disappeared into the back.

"Patty, how nice to see you," said Rose, smiling warmly. Patrice noticed dark circles under her eyes and a sallow cast to her normally glowing complexion. She had lost a lot of sleep.

Rose was where T.K. had gotten his golden-brown complexion from. He also had her eye color, but the rest—his build, his height, the shape of his nose and mouth—were more similar to his father's, who was still a handsome man in his late sixties.

"It's nice to see you, too, Mrs. McKenna," said Patrice sincerely. Rose was five-four to Patrice's five-seven, and she was on the stout side, like Patrice's mother. She was still in her robe and slippers.

"Have you heard anything?" Patrice asked.

Rose gestured for Patrice to follow her. Patrice assumed she was going to the kitchen, but Rose turned and went down the long hallway that led to the sunroom on the east side of the big house. It was considered Rose's room because that's where she kept her books and her desk. She considered herself a writer, and she loved to come in here every day and work on her stories. She had never been published. She said she didn't need the money or the notoriety, should success follow. She wrote for the sheer pleasure of writing. Patrice envied her just a little. To feel that passionate about her chosen avocation but not to seek payment for her efforts was either crazy or noble. In Rose McKenna's case, it was noble.

A tea service sat on the coffee table in front of the couch. "No, we haven't heard from Aisha. Please sit down," Rose said. She poured them cups of steaming tea and handed a cup to Patrice. "This always calms me when I'm under stress," Rose said softly. She sipped her tea and regarded Patrice with warm brown eyes so like T.K.'s that Patrice felt her stomach muscles contract painfully with regret.

"I heard how T.K. spoke to you last evening," Rose

said without preamble. "I hope you don't think that was really him talking. He was angry. It's not a state he's been in a lot. He usually handles things better. Well, you've spent time with him. You know how he is most of the time—a very sweet person."

Patrice nodded in agreement. "I was shocked to see him that way."

"I know you were. That's why I wanted to talk to you today." Rose set her cup down

She looked Patrice in the eyes. "Let me tell you about T.K. and Malcolm. T.K. looked out for Malcolm from the time we brought him home from the hospital. Malcolm was mentally challenged. He'd been that way since birth—a lack of oxygen. Growing up, T.K. protected him from neighborhood bullies, ignoring taunts from people who called his brother names, hateful things that no boy should have to hear. When T.K. started having some success as an actor, he sent for Malcolm even before he convinced me and his father to move here. Knowing we were aging, he wanted to take some of the responsibility of looking out for Malcolm off of us. I'm sure it cut into his personal life, but he didn't care. He wanted his brother out here with him. After we moved here, we wanted Malcolm to come live with us, but T.K. insisted that his brother was a man and shouldn't have to live with his parents. Malcolm liked that about T.K. He helped him feel independent. When Malcolm met Aisha and fell in love, we all hoped that it would work out. Yes, we noticed that money was going out of his accounts at an alarming rate, but if he was happy, we didn't want to step in and tell him to quit seeing Aisha. That's where T.K. thinks we were wrong. He blames himself for Malcolm getting involved with Aisha, and he blames himself for not being there when Malcolm got drunk and tried to drive while intoxicated. You see, Malcolm and Aisha had argued, he drank to forget and then in his drunken state he was going to see her."

"From Malibu to Los Angeles," Patrice said.

"Yes," Rose confirmed. She sighed sadly. "Fortunately, no one else was injured that night. Malcolm would have been devastated if he had hurt anyone. He was very kindhearted." Tears fell, and she wiped them away with a corner of a cloth napkin.

Patrice found herself crying in sympathy. Rose handed her a cloth napkin. "I like you, Patty," Rose told her. "I believe you're good for my son. He's not without his demons. We all have them, but he has a good heart, and I think he regrets how he spoke to you yesterday. Please try not to hold it against him."

Patrice was touched. Tears continued to fall, and she knew that was as much because she felt heartbroken over her altercation with T.K. as it was because she felt sympathy for a grieving mother.

Realistically, however, she knew his mother couldn't speak for T.K., so she took Rose McKenna's words with a grain of salt.

"Would you please shut that brat up?" shouted Kinesha Jackson, Aisha's mother. Kinesha had to be at work at eight o'clock, and it was five in the morning. The little apartment didn't have soundproof walls, so she heard every whimper from Mira. Aisha sat up on the lumpy couch. She and Mira had to sleep there because her mother wasn't about to give up her bed for them.

She held Mira in her arms and rocked her. "Shh, baby girl. It's okay. That mean, big-mouthed woman isn't going to get you." Mira continued to wail.

"I heard that, Aisha. You'd better mind your mouth or you and that bastard will be out on the street."

"You'd really put us out?" Aisha asked, incredulous. "You've never done anything for me and you'd put me out when I need your help the most?"

"Hell, yeah, I'd put you out. Now quiet down that rug rat," said Kinesha. "Somebody's got to work in this house."

"I told you that I'll get a job as soon as I find a day care for Mira," Aisha reminded her irascible mother.

"Sure, you will," said Kinesha. "The only job you ever kept was being kept." She laughed. "Too bad that stupid boy killed himself."

That was it for Aisha. She had taken her mother's snide remarks for eight days. She had put up with them because she didn't have anywhere else to go. But when she started talking that way about Malcolm, she had to speak up. "He was the nicest man I ever knew!" she screamed at her mother. Mira suddenly stopped crying. She looked up at her mother with beautiful black eyes in her brown face and smiled. Aisha smiled back. "That's right," she cooed. "Your father was a good man. And you know what? You look just like him. He didn't have an easy life. And it was his unlucky day when he met me because all I wanted was a meal ticket. But you know what? After a while, I fell in love with him. I really did." Now that Mira had stopped crying, she started. "I could have been nicer to him. I made him think he could never please me. I made him jump through hoops just to watch him jump. I was so selfish. It's my fault he's dead. I don't deserve you, little Mira. I really don't. I don't have my head right yet—not enough to be a good momma to you."

"Quit blubbering so I can get some sleep," Kinesha yelled.

Aisha lay back down with Mira cradled in her arms. "Soon, sweet girl, I'm taking you back where you'll be safe. That wicked witch is going to make me commit murder, and then where will you be?"

Mira smiled at her.

T.K. rolled over in bed and grabbed his cell phone from the nightstand. He dialed Patrice's number and listened to her voice on voice mail. Then he hung up. Yes, she would know he had phoned. He'd phoned plenty of times over the past nine days and either left a brief, impersonal message or had left no message at all. She wasn't returning his calls, and he couldn't blame her. Maybe she was giving him space, or maybe she had washed her hands of him. He'd never know unless he went over there, and he was still too embarrassed to do that. His mother had told him she'd come by to drop Sam and the car off and ask if they'd heard anything from Aisha.

He had still been reeling from what he perceived as her abandonment of him to notice that his mother was looking at him strangely. "Do you love her?" she'd abruptly asked him.

"I thought I did, but she's not who I thought she was," he'd said, sounding like a spoiled child now that he thought about it.

"Don't act like a fool," his mother had warned him. "Love doesn't come around that often. If we find it once we're lucky. If she's your once, you'd better stop being stubborn and ask her to forgive your asinine behavior."

"Must you talk like a schoolteacher?" he had joked, trying to lighten the mood.

"Oh, that word's meaning is easy to ascertain, it just means someone who's acting like an ass!" his mother had said, and left the room.

Now T.K. got out of bed and went into the bathroom. After using it, he washed his hands and went back to lie down. It was only seven in the morning. When he had phoned Patrice earlier, he'd had no fear of waking her. She got up and jogged at around this time. He lay with his hands locked behind his head. He was still at his parents' house. He would remain here until they found out where Aisha was.

The detective agency his lawyer had hired had not had

any luck. They had been on the job for a week now. He was disappointed, to say the least. He wanted to fire them and hire someone else, but his lawyer had told him they were the best on the West Coast. Somehow a woman with a two-month-old baby in tow had eluded them. Obviously Aisha had gone where no detective agency had gone before.

He fell back to sleep and was awakened two hours later by the ringing of his cell phone. He saw that it was Patrice. He answered instead of letting it go to its message function. "Hello," he said simply, his tone soft.

He heard a sharp intake of breath and nothing else. She had not expected him to answer. Nor had she been prepared to say anything. She was probably going to listen to his voice on voice mail and hang up just as he'd done. She sighed. He melted at the sound of her voice with only that one exhalation. "Have you heard anything from Aisha?" she asked.

He had to clear his throat before he could speak. "No, we haven't heard from her."

"I'm sorry," she said. "Um, I'd better go then."

"Wait!"

"Yes?"

"How are you?"

"I'm fine," she said.

"Were you out running when I called earlier?"

"Yes."

She wasn't going to make this easy for him. He cleared his throat again. "May I come over?"

"For what?" she asked, her tone inquisitive.

"To see you," he said.

"I have your email address. I'll send you a photo."

"For God's sake, Patty. I made a mistake. I've been a fool. I shouldn't have spoken to you that way. I panicked, and I wasn't thinking clearly. I thought that if you weren't with me, you were against me. I was wrong, as my mother has pointed out to me on numerous occasions. My lawyer gave me the same advice you did, not to contact the police."

This came as a surprise to her. "You haven't had the police out looking for her all this time? You hired a private detective?"

"That's all I could do," he said. "She's Mira's mother. She had every right to take her."

"She could still come back," Patrice told him, her voice hopeful.

He sighed deeply. "I hope so. It would kill me not to know what's happened to Malcolm's daughter." She heard his anguish, and her heart went out to him.

It was the same heart he had crushed though, and she knew if she saw him the next move would be to make love to him. "No, we shouldn't see each other right now," she told him. "Our emotions are still too raw. Come when you're positive your head and heart are in the right place—when your demons are dead or at least silenced. I'll wait for you."

Rose heard the doorbell while she was writing. She saved what she had written and slowly got up from the desk. Her arthritic knee was giving her some trouble today.

"Alma," she called as she walked toward the front door. "Are you getting that?"

There was no sign of Alma. She supposed she was downstairs in the laundry room. By the time she got to the door and looked through the peephole, whoever had been there was gone. They lived in a gated community. The guard at the gate wouldn't allow anyone to come in unless they were on the list of authorized people. She felt safe to open her door and peer outside.

When she opened the door, there was Mira in her car seat, smiling up at her. Rose cried out in joy, "Mira!" She picked Mira up. She looked along the driveway and across the expanse of lawn, searching for Aisha, but there was no sign of her. "Aisha! Aisha! Come back! We're not angry! We're just happy to have you back!" She was hoping Aisha was hiding somewhere, but if the girl was still here, she didn't want to show herself. "If you can hear me, Aisha, thank you! We'll take care of her until you decide you're ready to come back for her."

With that, Rose McKenna took her granddaughter inside.

She placed the car seat on the foyer table and reached in to remove Mira from it. Her granddaughter was clean and sweet-smelling. Aisha had taken good care of her. She kissed her sweet face repeatedly. "Where have you been?" she asked, grinning.

Rose was at a loss. Her husband and her son were out.

She would have to call them with the news. The only person there to share in her joy was Alma. "Alma," she called. "Come see who's come back home after twelve days!"

When Alma showed up, she took one look at Mira and shouted, "Praise God!"

T.K. was pulling through his parents' front gates when he saw Aisha getting in the back of a taxi parked near the guard house. He gunned the motor and sped across the lawn, turned the car around, went up over the curb and arrived in time to block the taxi's exit. He jumped out of the car and slammed the door behind him. Going to Aisha's side of the car, he yanked her door open and pulled her out. "Hey, fella," the cab driver shouted, getting out of the car himself, "you can't do that." Then he saw whom he was addressing and grinned broadly. "Hey, you're T. K. McKenna. I've been drivin' people to Beverly Hills for years and never saw a star. You're my first."

T.K. ignored him. "Where is Mira!" he demanded of Aisha.

"She's with your mom," Aisha said, cowering. She thought he was going to hit her.

T.K. didn't believe her. He looked in the taxi, backseat and front seat. "I'm not letting you out of my sight until I see her," he told her. He dug in his pocket, got a fifty and gave it to the cab driver. "That'll cover it?"

"Yeah," said the cab driver. "Can I have an autograph, too?"

"Don't press your luck," said T.K. and dragged Aisha over to his car where he opened the passenger-side door, climbed in and dragged her inside the car with him. He shut the passenger-side door, locked the doors and then started the engine. A few moments later, he was at his parents' front door. He started to reach for Aisha again and she said, "You don't need to force me to come inside. I'll come."

She did as she'd promised, and they went into the house where they found Rose and Alma standing in the foyer. Rose had Mira in her arms, and Alma was fawning over her.

Rose looked up and smiled when she saw T.K. "I was getting ready to phone you," she told him, going to him and placing Mira in his arms.

At first, she hadn't noticed Aisha because she was hanging back, nervous about the reception she might get. T.K.'s behavior toward her hadn't lessened her fears.

When she saw the frightened girl, Rose went to her and pulled her into her arms for a firm hug. "Let me apologize," she said. "It wasn't our intention to make you think we were going to take Mira away from you. We don't want that. A child should be with her mother."

Aisha sobbed in her arms. When she was finally able to pull herself together, she looked down into the woman's eyes who might have been her mother-in-law if things had gone differently. She was a kind woman, the best of women, the sort who routinely made sacrifices for their families, who had genuine love for their families.

Aisha had never known that. She was done with deluding herself, though. She couldn't blame her present life on her upbringing. She had to start living her own life sometime, and that sometime was right here and now.

"Don't apologize to me," she told Rose McKenna. "You were always good to me. I'm the one who should be apologizing. First of all, despite appearances, I really did love Malcolm, but I was so ignorant that I didn't know how to express that love or, really, how to accept it. I only learned to appreciate him after he was gone, and I'll always regret that. After he was gone, I kind of lost it. I was pregnant and had no way of supporting us. I felt desperate. That's why I behaved the way I did with T.K. I'm sorry for that. And I'm sorry for disappearing the way I did, but I *did* think you were going to take Mira away from me, and I felt helpless to defend myself. You can afford the best lawyers, and I don't even have a home to call my own. I panicked and went to stay with my mom for a few days, but she made it clear that we weren't welcome there. You were the only ones I knew who would make sure Mira got the care she needed. So I set her on the front stoop, rang the bell and ran."

T.K. was listening to all of this while he held his niece and gazed lovingly into her sweet face. He walked over to Aisha and placed Mira in her arms. "From this point on, you're a part of the family. That's what I should have told you from the beginning when I asked you to come live here, but I had my own demons to wrestle with." He didn't elaborate. He looked her in the eyes.

"Malcolm would want both you and Mira to be taken care of. Whatever hell you've been through, it's over now. You're home."

Aisha cried anew and kissed her daughter's forehead. "I'm going to be a good mother. You'll see."

"You're already a good mother," T.K. said simply. "Now, if you ladies will excuse me, I have to go somewhere."

Patrice had started running more, sometimes twice a day. She would split up the distance, running two miles in the morning and two in the evening. She had completed her evening run and had walked the last few blocks home when she saw T.K. standing on her porch. She was taking her pulse rate as she walked, and when she saw him, it sped up. She stopped at the gate and looked at him. "I hope you have good news."

He smiled, and she knew that he did. "Mira and Aisha are safe. She brought her back a few minutes ago."

She closed the distance between them, strolling up the brick walkway that led to the porch and joined him on it. "Then why aren't you at home?" she asked.

T.K. was so full of emotion that he was afraid that if he uttered one more word he would start crying like a baby. He didn't want her to see him that way. He'd missed her so much that it took every ounce of willpower he had not to grab her and kiss her breathless.

She put a hand on his strong forearm and felt the

coiled power within him, the pent up longing. "Why aren't you with your family?" she asked again.

"I am," he said.

Patrice laughed softly. Relief flooded her body, and with it came tears. She went into his arms. T.K. clung to her tightly, and she felt his body shudder as if he hadn't been certain she would forgive him. She peered into his eyes and said, "I love you so much," and then she kissed him.

When they raised their heads to look into each other's eyes, T.K. said, "I was so full of guilt for not being there for Malcolm the night he got into that car and tried to drive to L.A. drunk, that I couldn't see clearly. And as it turned out, Aisha really loved him, and she went a little nuts after he died, not knowing what was to become of her or Mira. That's why she tried to blackmail me into marrying her or else she'd take Mira and disappear. We both had demons to exorcise." He took a deep breath, and kissed her forehead. Looking deeply into her eyes, he said, "Let's get married today."

Patrice grinned. "As much as I like the sound of that, I'm pretty sure we need to get a license and a few other things done before we can do that."

Seeing the determined look in his eyes, she laughed. "You mean, Vegas, don't you?"

He nodded in the affirmative.

Patrice laughed again and began backing away from him as though he'd lost his mind. "Oh, no, I'm not getting married in a Vegas chapel. My parents would be highly disappointed."

"They'll get over it," T.K. said as he swept her into his arms and carried her down the steps of the porch.

"This is kidnapping!" Patrice exclaimed happily.

"This is love," T.K. corrected her.

* * * * *

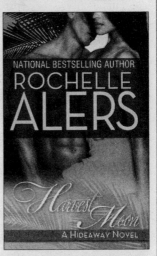

REQUEST YOUR FREE BOOKS!

2 FREE NOVELS
PLUS 2 *FREE GIFTS!*

KIMANI™
ROMANCE

Love's ultimate destination!

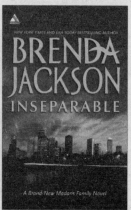